Martha shone the light on a tombstone almost hidden under the bush that had grown up around it. Tracing the letters with her finger, she read, "In loving memory of our beloved son, Thomas Livingston, gone but not forgotten. 14 April 1868–18 June 1874."

"So?" Steven looked at her. "I mean it's sad and all that, but what's it got to do with the tunnel?"

"Look at the bush, Steven," Martha went on. "It practically covers the tombstone. I bet you anything that tunnel ends in Thomas Livingston's grave."

Other novels by
Mary Downing Hahn

The Thirteenth Cat
Guest
The Girl in the Locked Room
One for Sorrow
Took
Where I Belong
Mister Death's Blue-Eyed Girls
Time for Andrew
The Ghost of Crutchfield Hall
Closed for the Season
All the Lovely Bad Ones
Deep and Dark and Dangerous
Witch Catcher
The Old Willis Place
Hear the Wind Blow
Anna on the Farm
Promises to the Dead
Anna All Year Round
As Ever, Gordy
Following My Own Footsteps
The Gentleman Outlaw and Me—Eli
Look for Me by Moonlight
The Doll in the Garden
The Wind Blows Backward
Stepping on the Cracks
The Spanish Kidnapping Disaster
The Dead Man in Indian Creek
December Stillness
Following the Mystery Man
Tallahassee Higgins
Wait Till Helen Comes
The Jellyfish Season
Daphne's Book
The Time of the Witch
The Sara Summer

THE PUPPET'S PAYBACK

and Other Chilling Tales

MARY DOWNING HAHN

Clarion Books
Houghton Mifflin Harcourt
Boston   New York

Some of the stories in this book were published
previously in slightly different forms:
"The Last House on Crescent Road" appeared in
Don't Give Up the Ghost, ed. David Gale. Delacorte Press, 1993.
"The Grounding of Theresa" appeared in
Bruce Coville's Book of Ghosts. Scholastic, 1994.
"Give a Puppet a Hand," now called "The Puppet's Payback," appeared in
Bruce Coville's Book of Nightmares. Scholastic, 1995.
"Trouble Afoot" appeared in
Bruce Coville's Book of Monsters, II. Scholastic, 1996.

Clarion Books is an imprint of
Houghton Mifflin Harcourt Publishing Company.

hmhbooks.com

The text was set in Palatino.
Cover design by Opal Roengchai
Interior design by Opal Roengchai

Library of Congress Cataloging-in-Publication Data is available.

ISBN: 978-0-358-06732-0 hardcover
ISBN: 978-0-358-53978-0 paperback

Manufactured in the United States of America
1 2021
4500829774

For Dinah,
with thanks for helping me tell my stories

CONTENTS

THE NUMBER SEVEN BUS

O ne day last spring, I decided to skip school. It was a warm, sunny day, one of the first nice days of the year, and the air smelled like fresh-cut grass and lilacs —much too great a day to spend at Hiram Adams Middle School, slaving away for a bunch of sadistic teachers who loved to make kids feel stupid and worthless. Besides, I hadn't studied for my biology test or written my book report for language arts. It made sense to hang out at the lakefront, doing stunts on my skateboard, instead of sitting in a classroom.

Sometime in the afternoon, the weather changed, the way it often does in March. The sky darkened, the wind blew, and the rain came cutting through the air sideways, soaking me to the skin. I grabbed my skateboard and headed for the mall. I'd dry out playing a few rounds of *Storm Blaster* at the arcade and then take the bus home. If I timed it right, I'd get there before Mom came back from work. She'd never guess I hadn't been in school.

It would probably have worked if I hadn't lost track of time. Once I start playing a game like *Storm Blaster*, I totally forget the rest of the world, especially if I'm on a winning streak. I'm in the game. I'm part of it, breathing the same air as the hero, seeing what he sees, hearing what he hears, doing what he does. Mom often said the world could end and I'd miss it completely.

Anyway, the next thing I knew, five hours had vanished. It was nine thirty, and the mall was closing. Now I was in for it. I hadn't called Mom, who would be a nervous wreck—and furious as well.

On my way out of the arcade, I reached into my pocket for my phone. It wasn't where I usually keep it, so I checked every pocket twice before I remembered I'd left it at home, charging. What was I going to tell Mom? I'd gone to the library? I'd stayed after school to watch a basketball game? I'd gone to Mike's house to play *Storm Blaster* on his Nintendo Switch? I was thinking so hard I bumped right into this guy who was also leaving the arcade.

"Sorry," I said, taking a step to the side.

"Be more careful next time," he said in a menacing voice.

I opened my mouth to come back with a smart remark

but changed my mind when I realized who he was. I'd seen him in the arcade before, always alone, playing in a dead earnest way that made me seem like a goof-off. Strange-looking too — tall and gaunt and ashy pale, wearing a black T-shirt and jeans, his dark hair in a long ponytail. He had sleeve tattoos on both arms. He was definitely one weird dude, the kind who belongs to a motorcycle gang, the kind who's not quite normal — the kind you don't want to mess with.

Gripping my skateboard a little tighter, I edged away and headed for the bus stop outside the mall's west entrance. It was dark, not raining hard but misting just enough to blur everything. The mall and the parking lot were both emptying fast. I glanced over my shoulder. No sign of the guy from the arcade.

A normal-looking kid was sitting on the bench, obviously waiting for a bus.

"Has Number Seven come yet?" I asked him.

"You just missed it, man," he said, looking at his watch. "There should be another one in about ten minutes though. They come pretty regularly at closing time."

That wasn't great news. The temperature had dropped way down since I'd left home. I was freezing to death in my stupid short-sleeved T-shirt.

The boy got on Number Eight, and I sat on the bench alone, but not for long. By the time good old Number Seven pulled into sight, I'd been joined by three or four other people. We all crowded through the door, joking about the change in the weather and stuff like that. I dropped into a seat near the back. With any luck, I'd be home in half an hour. That gave me thirty minutes to come up with a good story for Mom.

Just before the driver shut the door, the guy from the arcade got on the bus. He sat down across the aisle from me, one row up. He wasn't doing anything out of the ordinary, but I kept looking at the back of his head. I can't explain it. There was just something so strange about him.

After about five minutes, he turned and caught me looking at him. I'd never seen eyes like his. They were almost colorless, making it hard to tell where the iris ended and the white began. His pupils were black dots, smaller than a period at the end of a sentence printed in the tiniest type. Worst of all, his unblinking stare cut right through my eyes to the thoughts hidden in my head. Or at least it felt that way.

He sneered and turned back around, allowing me to look away at last. My heart pounded, my breath came in ragged little gasps, and my mouth filled with hot spit the way it does just before you throw up. Pressing my face against the window, I peered outside. We were two blocks from the corner where I always got off. Never had Pearce Street looked darker, lonelier—not a person in sight, not many streetlights, mainly because my friends and I had gone on a spree with our air rifles and used them for target practice.

I glanced at the guy. Just as I'd feared, he was half turned toward me again, watching me. Before he looked away, a smirk lifted the corner of his mouth.

What if he followed me off the bus? I had five long, dark blocks to walk before I reached my house.

When the driver stopped at Pearce Street, two or three people got off, but I decided to stay where I was. At the end of the line, the guy would make his exit—he'd have to. Once he was gone, I'd sweet-talk the driver into letting me ride back to Pearce Street. I was a kid. No adult would make me walk three or four miles in the dark. Of course, I'd get home even later, but Mom was a whole lot easier to face than this weird guy, whoever he was.

When we reached the terminus, only the guy and I were on the bus. The driver opened the door, and the guy got off. He glanced back once like he was surprised not to see me following him. I grinned and waved, pleased I'd fooled him, and he walked off into the shadows.

"Hey, kid." The driver had gotten to his feet and was frowning at me. "This is the end of the line. Didn't you hear me? Everybody off."

I walked down the aisle, looking out the windows to scan the darkness. No sign of him. But then, he'd be hard to see dressed in those black clothes.

"I missed my stop," I said, giving him my most charming smile, the one I saved for special occasions in the principal's office. "Fell asleep or something. If it's okay, sir, I'll ride back with you as far as Pearce Street."

"Sorry, kid," the driver said, obviously unmoved by my manners, which would have amazed most adults, Mom included. "Let this be one of life's little learning experiences. Stay awake next time."

"But you don't understand," I said. "My house is three or four miles from here. It's late. It's dark out there . . ."

The driver shook his head. "Don't tell me a tough kid like you is afraid of the dark."

I hated that kind of smart talk from adults, but I was in no position to tell him what I thought of rude bus drivers. "Listen," I said, "did you see the guy who got off here?"

The driver yawned without bothering to cover his mouth. "I didn't notice him."

"He was sitting right there." I pointed at the empty seat where he had been. "Tall and skinny, with a long, scraggly ponytail, wearing a black T-shirt and black jeans, kind of weird-looking."

"Oh, him." The driver shrugged. "He rides this route all the time. What about it?"

"Well, he followed me out of the arcade at the mall." I was beginning to feel a little dumb. Was I blowing this way out of proportion? "He kept looking at me," I added, feeling even dumber.

"I can't imagine why he'd waste his eyesight on you," the driver said, showing off his great wit. "Besides, he's never caused me any trouble. We come to the end of the line, and he gets off. Like any normal person."

"Look," I said, trying not to whine like a little kid, "just let me ride back to Pearce Street. That's all I'm asking you."

"Even if I wanted to, I couldn't," the driver said. "This is the last bus, kid. I've been driving for eight hours. All I want to do now is go home and have a beer."

Cursing myself for not thinking of this possibility, I

followed the driver across a dark parking lot to a beat-up old Ford Camaro parked under a streetlight.

"Then give me a ride home," I begged. "Please."

The driver unlocked his car door. "No dice, kid. Pearce Street is miles out of my way."

"My mom will pay you for your trouble, I guarantee it."

He shook his head and got into the car. Before I could stop him, he slammed the door in my face. Dropping my skateboard, I ran around to the passenger side, but the door was locked. Rolling the window down half an inch, he said, "I never give rides to strangers."

Gunning the motor, he drove away.

"Wait!" I ran after the car, yelling for him to stop, but he kept going. In seconds, the Camaro's taillights vanished around a corner, and I was standing in the middle of the street all by myself.

No, not all by myself. The guy in black had stepped out of the shadows a few feet ahead of me. He stood with his hands on his hips, his head tilted, as tense as a cat watching a bird.

I whirled around and started running in the opposite direction, but no matter which way I ran, he was always ahead of me, grinning that terrible grin. When I was too exhausted to take another step, he came right up to me and seized my shoulders. His fingers chilled me to the bone.

"What's the use, Matthew?" he asked. "You can't get away from me. Quit trying."

"How do you know my name?" I whispered.

"I've been watching you and your friends for a long time. I know all your names — Tony, Mike, Travers, and you, Matthew." As he spoke, he held my eyes with his. "I've been hoping to get one of you alone, and look — here you are."

"Do you want money? Is that it? I haven't got a cent on me, but I live right there." I pointed a shaky finger at the closest house. A light shone from the front window. I figured if I ran up the steps and banged on the door, someone would let me in. They'd call the police, call my mother, save me from this guy. "My mother will be glad to —"

He shook his head. "Don't lie to me, Matthew. I know where you live. I've followed you and your friends more than once. And none of you ever saw me."

I tried again to pull away, but he held my shoulders so tight my bones ached. I yelled for help, but nobody came to a window or opened a door.

The guy pressed his hand over my mouth. "Be quiet," he said. "Why struggle? You're mine now."

"Let me go," I pleaded. "Please. My mother—"

"Not till you give me what I want." He bared his teeth, and I knew what he was.

"No," I whispered, "no, you can't be real, you—"

"Oh, but I am real," he murmured softly. "In fact, I'm the realest thing you'll ever meet."

With that, he leaned over me and sank his fangs into my neck. The world spun into darkness, and I spun with it, sinking down, down, into nothing.

You probably thought that was the end of me. I wouldn't blame you. I sure thought so at the time. But the funny thing is I'm still around. Not that anyone knows.

Mom visits my grave at least once a week to shed a few tears for me, her poor son. I feel bad for her. I'd love to tell her what's really going on, but she wouldn't understand. She might even try to do something about it. After all, she and I watched a lot of horror movies together. There's not much she doesn't know about silver crosses and wooden stakes and garlic.

Some of my old friends drop by too. We always liked skateboarding in the cemetery, so they make a point of passing my grave and doing special stunts for me. They'd never guess I'm applauding every fancy move they make.

Only Vince knows the truth. He comes for me after dark, wearing his black T-shirt and jeans, whistling me out of my cozy lead-lined coffin. He's not such a bad guy once you get to know him.

We hang out at the arcade, keeping in the shadows, taking care not to be recognized. He's taught me all he knows about the games, as well as a few other things. I'm learning fast, he says, just like he thought I would.

When the mall closes, Vince and I always catch the last Number Seven bus. Keep your eyes open on your ride home. Maybe you'll see us one night and wonder who we are and why we're watching you. Don't be scared if we get off at your stop and follow you. It might take you a while, but trust me, you'll learn to like Vince and me and the way we live.

213 POPLAR STREET

Ever since school let out, I'd been in the library, working on an assignment for English. Just before the library closed, I picked up a stack of books and headed for the checkout desk.

Mrs. Fisher smiled and took the stack. "Just in time, William," she said. "We close in five minutes."

"It took me ages to find what I needed."

"Big assignment?"

I faked a groan and she laughed.

As soon as she was done with my books, I stuffed them into my backpack, zipped my jacket, and went outside to meet my sister, Lynn. She had the family car that night, and Mom had told her to pick me up when the library closed at six.

I looked up and down the street, but I didn't see our old Volvo. No surprise. Lynn was always late.

A few people left the library and hurried off into the dark. A fog had settled in, and they soon disappeared from view. While I stood on the steps shivering, the door behind me locked with an unmistakable click. A few minutes later, the lights inside went out. Then I heard cars starting in the parking lot behind the building. The librarians drove away, heading for home, but here I was, on the library steps all by myself, still waiting, still cold, and getting madder by the minute.

I walked to the curb and peered up and down the street. Because of the fog, I couldn't see very far in either direction, but our Volvo wasn't in sight.

I pulled out my cell phone to call Lynn and realized I'd forgotten to charge it. If I had to, I could walk home. I'd done it plenty of times in the daylight. Normally it took about half an hour, but between the dark and the fog, the familiar streets looked menacing, sinister, threatening. It was as if I were in a different town whose streets I didn't recognize.

I waited a little longer, but finally I gave up. Lynn wasn't coming. Shoving my hands in my pockets, I headed down Forty-Second Avenue. Streetlights glowed dimly, almost hidden in the fog. Bare winter trees loomed up as I approached and shrank away behind me. A woman walking her dog passed me and disappeared into the fog like a ghost.

It was a Sherlock Holmes night, perfect for a murder.

I heard footsteps behind me. I saw dim shapes emerging from the fog and then vanishing. I told myself no one had ever been murdered in Union Heights. Monsters and fiends didn't hide in shadowy yards. It was foggy and dark, that's all. I'd read too many scary books and seen too many scary movies. I was letting my imagination go crazy.

But still I walked faster, especially after I realized I'd taken the route home that passed the town cemetery. I knew it was crammed with dead people, their burials marked by crosses and tombstones and angels, all crowded together, slanting this way and that, some lying broken on the ground. Scary in the daylight, the graveyard was way scarier at night.

I crossed the street to avoid walking so close to it, but even at this distance, I saw the tombstones crowding up to the fence as if they were trying to squeeze between the bars and escape.

I sped up until I was almost running. The sooner I left the cemetery behind, the better.

Just as I neared the cemetery's tall gates, I heard a child crying—or at least that's what it sounded like. But how could a child be in the cemetery? It had to be something else, an animal probably. Our neighbor had a Siamese cat that sounded just like a baby when it cried.

Spooked by the sound, I walked faster. But I heard it again. And again. A small voice calling for help. Definitely not a cat.

Almost hidden in the fog, a little girl stood behind the cemetery's gate, clutching the bars like a prisoner.

"Please help me!" she cried. "I can't get out."

She sounded so desperate and looked so helpless, I crossed the street to speak to her. "How did you get into the cemetery?" I asked. "What were you doing in there after dark?"

She twisted a long strand of dark hair around her finger and looked worried. "It's my own fault, you see. I wandered away from my companions and took the wrong path, and now I cannot open the gate."

"Your friends left you here all by yourself?"

"Please," she begged. "Just open the gate and let me out. I can't bear to remain another moment in this dreadful place."

Although I expected the gate to be locked, I tugged and pulled, and slowly, with a loud grating and scraping noise, it opened just wide enough for the girl to slip out.

"Oh, thank you. Thank you. I am eternally grateful to you." She smiled up at me. "My name is Allegra. What is yours?"

"It's William."

"William." She thought a moment and smiled. "William is a good name. An honest sort of name. A boy with the name of William can be trusted."

It was a strange thing to say, but it was a compliment, I guessed. "I've never known anyone named Allegra," I said, "but I'm sure it's a good name too."

"I'm glad you think so."

Allegra took my hand. "The fog is so confusing," she said. "I'm not certain which way to go. May I ask you to walk me home? If it's not too much trouble, that is."

"It's no trouble at all. Where do you live?" Truthfully, walking her home would make me late for dinner, but how could I possibly leave a little girl to find her way all by herself?

"My house is number 213 Poplar Street. Do you know of it?"

"Of course I know where Poplar Street is. I've lived in this town all my life."

"All your life? My goodness. We never stay in one

place long." She held my hand tighter. "Is Poplar Street far from here?"

"Not too far. Just on the other side of the cemetery."

"I'd prefer not to walk beside the cemetery. May we go a different way?"

"Sure." She had no idea how glad she'd just made me. All the time we'd been standing by the gate, I'd been hearing strange sounds and spotting things moving among the tombstones. I knew my imagination was playing tricks on me again, but I was more than happy to put as much distance between us and the cemetery as possible.

Holding her hand, I led her to the corner and turned down Chestnut Street. As soon as the cemetery was out of sight, I took a deep breath and slowed down—no need to tire Allegra.

"Why did your friends leave you in the cemetery?" I asked her. "Were they trying to scare you or something? It seems like a mean thing to do to a kid as young as you. My sister would have been scared to death in a situation like that."

Allegra shrugged. "Oh, they're accustomed to my 'disappearing acts,' as they call them. I often wander off by myself. They know I'll either find my way home or someone like you will lead me there."

I stared at her, perplexed. She was the oddest girl I'd ever met. Most kids were scared of both the dark and cemeteries. But Allegra acted like it was no big deal to be abandoned on a dark, foggy night—in a cemetery no less.

"But it's so dark," I said, "and the fog is so creepy."

"Truly my companions would worry more about me being lost in the daylight than in the dark."

I laughed. "You have a weird sense of humor, Allegra."

She gave me an angry look. "I was not trying to be funny."

"I'm sorry. I just thought . . ." The frown on her face deepened, and I shut my mouth.

We walked on without talking. A passing car's lights illuminated Allegra's pale face. Without even glancing at me, she stared straight ahead, frowning as if she were still angry. After we'd walked another block in silence, I decided to ask her a question that couldn't possibly annoy her.

"Do you go to Hargrove Elementary School? My sister Rachel is in second grade. You must be around her age. Maybe you know her."

"I don't attend school. I have special lessons."

"Oh, you're homeschooled." That made sense. She probably spent a lot of time by herself. Maybe that explained why she spoke like someone in an old-fashioned book. And why she seemed way older than Rachel.

"Do you like staying home, instead of going to school?" I asked her.

"Sometimes I'd prefer to attend a real school. It's ever so lonely not to have friends."

"I could bring Rachel to your house. Maybe you'd like each other."

"That isn't possible. I am not allowed to socialize with other children."

"But what about the kids you were with in the cemetery?"

Allegra laughed. "Oh my goodness. What a funny thought. Why do you think of my companions as children?"

"Well, most kids are friends with kids their own age —like Reilly and me or Rachel and Colleen." I paused in case she wanted to say something, but she contemplated her shoes, which were shiny and as fancy as her dress. "If your friends aren't children, how do you play with them? What do you do?"

"Your questions are growing extremely tiresome,

William." Allegra freed her hand from mine and ran up the street ahead of me. "How far is it to Poplar Street now?" she called over her shoulder.

"Wait!" I hurried after her, afraid I'd lose her in the fog.

She stopped and watched me run toward her. I couldn't tell if she was still mad.

"I'm sorry. I didn't mean to be tiresome," I told her, "but you're so mysterious. It must be past dinnertime. Won't your parents be worried about you?"

Allegra smiled that odd little smile of hers, just a slight upturn of her lips. "I told you I often wander. No one worries if I'm late. They know I can take care of myself."

"But what if a strange man had come along and seen you in the cemetery? The kind of men you hear about on the evening news . . . You know what I mean. It's dangerous for you to be out after dark by yourself."

"I said you needn't worry about me. Perhaps you should worry about yourself instead."

Allegra sounded annoyed again. I jammed my hands into my pockets and walked on beside her. "Why should I worry about myself?"

"Bad things happen to boys too."

"Not very often," I muttered. "Not in this town, anyway."

Allegra looked at me. "Bad things happen everywhere, William."

She sounded sad, like maybe she knew more about bad things than I did.

Taking my hand again, she asked, "Are we almost to Poplar Street?"

"It's only a couple more blocks," I told her. "Are you cold? Your dress doesn't look very warm."

"It's my favorite frock." Allegra smoothed the skirt. "Isn't it pretty?"

"Rachel would love to have one just like it."

"Your parents would have difficulty finding a dress of this quality. It was made in Paris, especially for me."

"Are you from France?" Coming from a foreign country might explain her peculiarities.

"I wasn't born there, if that's what you mean. We travel to Europe frequently."

"Lucky you. I've never been anywhere except California, for my grandmother's funeral."

Allegra sighed. "Traveling becomes tiresome after a while—packing, unpacking, boarding ships, leaving ships." She yawned as if even talking about it bored her.

"Well, when I grow up, I'm going to travel around the world, me and my friend Reilly. We'll never be bored."

Allegra shrugged. We stopped on a corner, and I read the street sign through the fog. "This is Poplar Street. Is your house to the left or the right?"

Allegra looked in both directions. "The fog is so thick. I'm not certain which way to go."

"Let's turn right. If the house numbers are bigger than 213, we'll turn around and go the other way."

Of course, it didn't turn out to be that easy. The houses on Poplar were the oldest in town. They were big and set far apart on wide lawns. Some had porch lights, some didn't. The fog made it hard to read the numbers. To make it worse, we blundered along for a block or two only to discover we'd gone the wrong way. Frustrated, we turned around and retraced our steps.

As we passed a particularly nice house, I said, "Mom would love to live on this street."

"Would you like to live here, William?"

"Probably not. Just think of all the leaves I'd have to rake and the grass I'd have to mow." I looked at her. "Do you like living here?"

"Sometimes. Perhaps I'd enjoy it more if I had a playmate."

"Lots of kids live in this neighborhood. Rachel is

friends with Colleen Davis, who lives one block over on Walnut Street. Do you know her?"

She shook her head and looked at me sadly. "I told you I'm not allowed to play with other children."

"But—"

"We have certain standards."

"You mean those kids aren't good enough to be your friends?"

Allegra scowled. "You're asking questions again, William." She sighed and stared at a house number. "217— we're almost there." She walked more slowly, her head down, and finally came to a complete stop beside a grove of pine trees that hid her house from sight.

"I thought you were in a hurry to get home," I said.

She seized my hand. "Do you like me, William?"

"Sure I do. Why wouldn't I?"

She looked at me so intensely I was uncomfortable. I'd never noticed how pale her eyes were and how small her pupils. Suddenly uneasy, I took a step backward.

Her stare grew harder, colder. "Suppose I'm not as sweet as you seem to think I am. Suppose I never needed you to rescue me or to walk me home. Suppose I've just been pretending all along."

I stared at Allegra, confused by the change in her. "Why would you pretend?"

She moved closer to me, and I took another step backward. "Suppose *you* are the one in danger." Her eyes caught the light of a streetlamp. They seemed to be paler.

"What are you talking about, Allegra? I don't understand."

Suddenly she turned away and freed me from the spell of her eyes. Without looking at me, she said, "You have been kind to me, William, but you must leave now. I am not your friend. You must not expect me to be what I cannot be."

"But, Allegra, don't you want me to come home with you? Your parents might be mad at you. I can explain why you're late."

"No!" she cried. "They must think I came home alone."

"I don't understand."

"Believe me, it's better not to understand." She made a strange clicking noise with her teeth, like the sound my cat makes when it sees a bird. "Go home! And don't come back!" She ran toward her house. The gate opened and clanged shut behind her.

Hoping the fog hid me, I followed Allegra as far as her gate. I watched her run up the front steps. I saw the door open. A shadowy figure drew Allegra inside. Before the door slammed shut, I heard a deep voice say, "You promised to find someone, Allegra—"

I stared at the closed door. The windows of the house were dark. The only sound was the murmuring of the pine trees behind me.

Finally, I gave up and walked away. Trudging along the familiar sidewalks, I felt lost even though I knew where I was.

Why had Allegra told me to run away and not come back? Was it some sort of game I didn't know how to play? She'd gotten into my head and disturbed me. Confused me. Maybe I'd imagined the whole thing. Maybe I'd never let anyone out of the cemetery, maybe I hadn't walked anyone home.

I was thinking so hard I didn't see the Volvo until it pulled up beside me and Dad opened the door.

"I've been driving all over town looking for you," he said. "Your mother is worried sick."

When we got home, I told Mom my phone was dead and I'd gotten lost in the fog. I'm not sure why I didn't mention Allegra. I just didn't think I could explain how strange she was.

• • •

The next day, I decided to go to Allegra's house. I pictured myself knocking on the door and telling her parents I'd brought Allegra home last night. I'd say I wanted to see her again. The worst her parents could do was slam the door in my face and tell me not to come back. But there was a chance I'd see Allegra in her yard or at a window and we could talk. She was a mystery I needed to solve.

When I reached Poplar Street, I headed down the sidewalk toward number 213. When I reached the grove of pine trees, I stopped and went over what I'd say when I met Allegra's parents.

Hoping I'd figured out the right thing to tell them, I walked past the trees and stopped so fast I almost fell over my own feet.

Where the lawn should have been, I saw a field of dead weeds. Overgrown bushes hid the porch. Boards covered the windows. The roof sagged. The siding was bare weathered wood. The chimney leaned to one side.

Thinking I'd come to the wrong address, I walked to the next house and checked the number—*215*, in brass numerals over the front door.

I turned back and pushed the rusty gate open; *213* was painted on one of the pillars on the front porch. The paint on the door was cracked and peeling like dead skin. Piles of leaves lay in drifts against the splintered porch railings.

When I lifted the knocker, it came off in my hand. So I pounded on the door. "Is anyone home?" I shouted. "It's me, William."

"Hey!" somebody yelled. "Didn't you see the 'No Trespassing' sign?"

I turned around. A kid stood on the sidewalk scowling at me. I'd seen him at school, but he was a year ahead of me, and I didn't know his name.

I pushed through the weeds and joined him on the sidewalk. "Sorry, I didn't see the sign. Do you know who lives here?"

"Ghosts," the boy said. "It's haunted." He laughed. "At least that's what some people say. Me, I don't believe in that stuff."

"But I was here last night. I brought a little girl to this house. She said she lived here."

"She must have been playing a prank. Nobody's lived there for years. It ought to be torn down, but Dad says there's some problem with the deed."

"Her name is Allegra. Do you know her?"

"I know every kid on Poplar Street. I can tell you there's

nobody named Allegra." He slapped my back. "Hey, see you later. Got to go—soccer practice."

When he was out of sight, I walked around the corner and saw an alley running between Allegra's house and the one behind it. On the Poplar Street side of the alley, a tall weather-beaten fence hid everything but the top story of 213, but I found a gap big enough to squeeze through.

The house looked even worse from the back. The same tall weeds filled the yard. Almost hidden in them was what looked like the ruins of an old carriage. Junk of all sorts was scattered everywhere, shingles from the roof, boards and bricks, bottles and cans, a broken chair, a cracked mirror. It looked like people had been throwing their trash over the fence for years.

A trapdoor to the cellar was wide open, like an invitation to come inside. The steps sagged and one was missing, but I climbed down carefully. The stale air stank of mold and mildew and damp earth.

For a moment, I stood still, almost afraid to move. The place had a bad feeling, as if terrible things had happened there. Sorrow and misery and dark thoughts floated in the air. I imagined them clinging to my skin and hair and clothes.

I looked over my shoulder at the sky outside the cellar door. I should have climbed back up the steps and gone home, but I was too obsessed with finding Allegra to be sensible.

I groped my way through the cellar. Bottles rolled under my feet. Boxes split open in the damp air spilled moldy books and papers everywhere. A rusty furnace big enough to heat the world crouched in a dark corner.

At last I found the stairs to the first floor and climbed them slowly, one at a time, feeling my way upward. I knew by now that Allegra couldn't possibly be here, but maybe she'd left something behind that would tell me where she'd gone—or who she was.

The door at the top of the steps was warped. Pushing hard, I forced it open and almost fell into a hallway. Boarded-up windows let in some light, and I made my way into what must have been the parlor. Dust covered the floor, as thick as a gray carpet. Piles of dead leaves lay in the corners. The walls were streaked and stained and crumbling. Mice scrabbled inside the walls. Cobwebs swayed in a breeze, and the bones of small animals and birds who'd died in this place littered the floor.

In the dining room, a large table was set for dinner.

Carved wooden chairs surrounded it, some tipped over, some still standing. A huge chandelier draped with cobwebs hung from the sagging ceiling.

Faded paintings hung crooked on the walls; rotting curtains draped the windows; rusty pots and pans and broken dishes filled the kitchen sink; books in heaps lay on the floor, ruined with mildew.

I tiptoed up a grand staircase to the second floor. The bedrooms were like the rooms below, full of broken, dusty furniture. Rain had poured down the walls from holes in the roof, leaving heaps of crumbling plaster and decayed wallpaper.

In one small room, I found a child-size bed and rocking chair. An old doll sprawled in a corner, her hair gone and her dress in rags. One eye was open and the other shut. She looked like a dead child.

I went back downstairs. In the parlor, a thick photograph album lay open on the floor. I kneeled and turned its pages slowly, lingering on each faded face as if I might find a clue to the history of this house. I looked at mustached men wearing dark suit jackets over stiff-collared shirts, ties knotted at their throats, their hair neatly parted in the middle; women in fancy dresses with huge puffy sleeves, their hair hidden by large feathered hats;

and babies in long white dresses, boys in sailor suits, girls wearing dresses like the one Allegra had worn. A "frock," she had called it. A frock made in Paris especially for her.

After turning page after page, I found Allegra. Written beside her photograph was her full name: Allegra Amelia Sinclaire. On either side of her were people identified as her father and mother, both standing straight and looking serious.

Allegra looked just as I remembered her. In fact, she was wearing the same dress. I stared at her face, willing her to tell me how we'd met last night. She'd spoken to me. She'd walked with me to this very house. How could she be among the long-dead people in this album? Had I met her ghost? I shivered at the very idea, but how else could I explain it?

Looking for another photograph of her, I turned the album page. What I saw answered my questions. Captured forever in a faded picture, Allegra lay in a coffin, her eyes closed, her hands clasped over her chest. Her long curls framed her pale face, and she was dressed in her Paris frock.

Beneath was an inscription, faded but legible: *Allegra Amelia Sinclaire, beloved only child of Alexander and Emily*

Sinclaire, departed this earth on 12 June 1898 at the age of seven years, three months, and 27 days. She is now at rest with the Lord's holy angels.

On the facing page was a photograph of Allegra's burial place. An angel with drooping wings guarded the grave.

Looking closely, I made out the plot and row number that identified the grave's location in the town cemetery.

I don't know how long I sat there, cross-legged on the floor, staring at Allegra in her coffin. Finally, I pulled all three photographs from the album and put them in my pocket.

Shoving the front door until it screeched open, I squeezed through and ran down Poplar Street.

A sensible person would have gone straight home, but even though the sun was low in the sky, I headed for the cemetery to see Allegra's grave for myself.

After studying a map near the cemetery's front gate, I set out to find her grave among the wilderness of tombstones stretching out ahead of me. I was surrounded by the dead. Some of their memorials had fallen to pieces on the ground, crosses tilted to one side or another, angels missing wings or arms, their faces blank. Hundreds of graves, maybe thousands, lay in long crooked rows. I'd never realized how many people were buried here — more of them than us, I thought.

At last, Allegra's angel, the one I'd seen in the album, loomed ahead of me. The inscription had faded with time but was still clear enough to read: *Here lies Allegra Amelia Sinclaire, beloved only child of Alexander and Emily Sinclaire, departed this earth on 12 June 1898 at the age of seven years, three months, and 27 days. She is now at rest with the Lord's holy angels.*

Even with the evidence before me, I still couldn't believe that the girl I'd met last night lay beneath the ground at my feet. Yeah, she'd seemed sort of peculiar in the way she talked and dressed, but I'd never suspected her of being anything but a girl who needed help.

"Are you really buried here?" I asked Allegra. "Are you really dead?" I swear I half expected her to answer, maybe even to rise from the ground and tell me it was just a prank. But all I heard was the wind high in the treetops, and all I saw was her angel, its face almost worn away by time and its wings stained from years of rain.

Even though the sun had nearly set, I stayed there,

staring like a fool at Allegra's grave. "I just want to under-stand," I whispered. "I just want to know who or what you are."

She didn't answer, but I kept asking her questions. "Why did you choose me to walk you home? Why did you practically chase me away from your house? Don't you know I just wanted to help you?"

At last, I gave up. Allegra was gone. I'd never under-stand what happened last night. When I turned to go home, the sun had sunk below the trees, and the glow it left behind was fading from pink to gray. The tombstones between me and the gate seemed to have grown taller and moved closer to each other.

The evening air was cold and damp, and I was afraid. What if the gate was locked? What if I had to spend the night with the countless dead?

Stumbling over footstones and roots, I searched for the wide pathway that led to the gate, but darkness fell so fast I could barely see. No matter which way I turned, I found myself standing at the feet of Allegra's angel.

How was I to get out of the cemetery? Was I trapped here forever?

"It seems you are the one to need guidance tonight, William."

I looked up and saw Allegra. The moon was shining now. I'd wanted to see her a little while ago, but now she scared me—not because she looked different, but because I was no longer sure what she was.

She moved closer. "Why did you return, William? Did I not warn you to stay away?"

Scared of her shiny eyes, I backed away from her. "I went to your house. I looked for you. I found these." I pulled the photographs out of my pocket, and she took them. "Tell me what they mean."

She ignored me. The pictures held her attention.

I studied her pale face, her strange eyes, her long dark hair, her silk dress. Seeing her in moonlight instead of fog, I noticed she had no shadow. "Why did you ask me to help you find your way home? You knew where it was all the time."

"Truly, William, do you never stop asking questions?"

"Do you never answer them?"

Allegra shrugged. "Perhaps it's better for you not to know my secrets."

"Are you a ghost?"

"Why do you ask?"

"Because I want to know what you are. I want to understand."

"William, you are vexing me."

"Just tell me the truth for once."

"Perhaps I should introduce you to the companions I travel with. When you see them, you might understand what I am."

Without giving me a choice, she whistled three times —short, harsh notes like nothing I'd ever heard.

From the tombstones behind Allegra, three dark shapes rose up, veiled with black cloth so I couldn't see their faces.

"We are hungry for life," Allegra said, "my companions and I." Her voice dropped low, and I noticed her eyes again, how pale they were, how they glittered. "Are you frightened, William?"

Her companions surrounded me. They smelled like the basement in the house on Poplar Street—musty, old, like earth when you dig it up. And they made the same chittering sound that I'd heard Allegra make.

Allegra stepped closer to me, and I stepped back until I bumped up against a tombstone. "Why did you not listen to me?" she asked. "I warned you."

I held out my hands to keep her from coming closer. "I wanted to help you, Allegra."

"You entered the house where I died and disturbed the silence unbroken since my mother went to her grave."

"I needed to find you. I needed to understand where you'd gone."

Without listening to me, Allegra went on. "You opened the photograph album. You learned what you wanted to know. But instead of being satisfied, you stole my pictures and came here to bother me with endless questions that must never be answered."

Allegra turned to her companions. "What do you think should be done with this boy, this William, this annoyance?"

Without hesitating, they answered with one deep voice. "You brought us food late last night, dear child. We ate well and have no hunger. No one will miss the one you gave us, an old man who lived in the streets, but this boy has family and friends. Harming him may bring trouble to us. We say let him go."

The companions melted away into the night, leaving Allegra and me alone.

"Surely you understand now, foolish boy." Allegra smiled, and for the first time, I saw her teeth. "Why are you lingering, William? Do you not value your life?"

Like her companions, Allegra stepped into the shadows without making a sound. No twig snapped, no leaf stirred. She simply vanished.

Taking a deep breath, I ran faster than I'd ever run. Allegra and her companions might be playing with me like cats play with mice—let them go, let them run, let them think they're safe. Then pounce. Kill. Eat.

When I reached the road looping through the cemetery, I picked up speed. The gates were straight ahead. They were closed, just as I'd feared. This late, they were sure to be locked.

I threw my entire weight against them. They creaked and groaned but refused to yield. I turned sideways and tried to squeeze between the bars, but I couldn't get through.

I looked behind me again. The shadows were moving, even though no wind blew.

"Help!" I cried. "Help me!"

Light flashed from the guardhouse window. A man came out and pointed a flashlight at me. "What are you doing in there?" he yelled.

"Just unlock the gate, please, and let me out!"

Pulling a ring of keys from his pocket, he fumbled through them until he found the right one. "You must be another of them kids getting initiated. What club is it this time?"

The gate opened, and I almost fell into his arms.

The guard laughed. "Your pals said you had to spend the night in the graveyard, didn't they? And you took the dare. And look at you now, scared out of your wits."

I didn't answer, didn't even thank him. I ran across the street and kept going until I'd put several blocks between myself and the cemetery. Winded, I collapsed against a tree trunk and struggled to catch my breath.

I knew I'd be in trouble when I got home. I had no idea what sort of story I'd come up with, but I didn't care. All I wanted was the safety of my house, my room, my bed.

A few years later, when I was a senior in high school, number 213 Poplar Street was torn down. Apparently, the deed to the property had been settled, and the town council had unanimously voted to demolish the house.

To the neighborhood's shock, the construction workers found several skeletons in the basement. Although the police investigated, they never found the killer or identified the bones.

Kids at school thought the cops were covering something up. They made wild guesses about vampires and the living dead. Even though they claimed not to believe their own stories, they scared themselves. They slept with the lights on and stayed away from dark alleys.

I was the only one who knew that their guesses weren't far from the truth.

THE GROUNDING OF THERESA

The first thing I noticed about him wasn't his height or the color of his hair or even his clumsiness. It was the sound of his basketball shoes hitting the asphalt— *thud, thud, thud*. The noise was loud enough to wake the dead. His shadow drew my attention next. It was so much faster than he was, darting here and there, shortening and lengthening, fading and darkening as he moved in and out of the light. For several minutes, I leaned against the wall and watched his clumsy attempts to get the ball through the hoop clean and neat.

When I couldn't stand it any longer, I cleared my throat to let him know he wasn't alone on the court. I must have startled him because he whirled around so fast he dropped the ball. It bounced toward me, and I picked it up, loving the pebbly feel of it in my hands. It had been a long time since I'd played, but I hadn't forgotten. Dribbling close and tight, I ran toward him, leaped, and shot. The ball swished through the hoop without touching the rim.

The boy caught it on the rebound. "Nice shot," he said.

"Thanks." We stared at each other for a moment, two strangers on the school basketball court, his face lit by the white glare of a streetlight, mine hidden in the shadow of my baseball cap. Without saying a word, we started to play.

I gave him a real workout, feinting, blocking, stealing the ball, making one perfect shot after another. The August night was hot, muggy, hazy with air pollution. It bothered him a lot more than it did me. In no time he was breathing hard and soaked with sweat—hair, T-shirt, shorts, everything was wet. Too tired to concentrate, he made a wild throw. When the ball missed the backboard, he sat down on the asphalt and watched it bounce away into the darkness beyond the light.

"That's it for me," he muttered.

Even though he should have retrieved the ball, I ran after it, dribbled across the court, and shot one more perfect basket.

The ball rolled to his feet, but he didn't get up. "Don't you ever miss?"

I sat down beside him, breathing in his nice smell, and shrugged. "I'm pretty good."

He scowled. "Pretty conceited too."

I shrugged again. "I'm just telling the truth. No sense being modest."

He stared at me, taking in every detail of my appearance. I was glad I was sitting just out of the light's range. "How come I've never seen you before?" he asked. "Are you new in town?"

"I've been here awhile." I kept my answer vague on purpose, hoping to discourage more questions, but my ploy didn't work. He wanted to know how long I was staying, where I was from, what my parents did, all sorts of stuff that was none of his business. The only thing I told him was my name—T.J. Jones.

His name was Graham Mason. He was twelve years old, and he lived at the end of Adams Street. He was starting eighth grade in the fall, and he wanted to go out for basketball.

"The trouble is, I'm short for my age," he said. "Most of the guys are taller than I am. It gives them a certain advantage, you know what I mean? So I practice every night. Tryouts aren't till next month, and I figure I might get good enough by then if I really work at it."

"It's not just your height, Graham. Look at me. I'm short too, but I can play circles around you."

My honesty earned me another scowl. To soften my

words, I added, "It's not your fault. Some people have a special gift. They're naturally good at things. Maybe there's something you can do that I'm lousy at. Singing, maybe, or art—I can't carry a tune or draw a straight line."

"It so happens I'm the best artist in my grade." Graham was just as immodest as I'd been.

"There you go," I said. "You should practice drawing and forget basketball."

"I'm not interested in being an artist. I want to be a basketball player. I want people to cheer for me. I want them to get up on their feet and shout my name. 'Go, Graham, go!'"

I cocked my head and listened to the echo bounce off the school wall. It sounded like a whole crowd out there, cheering him on. He heard it too. I knew he saw himself running down the court, doing a perfect lay-up, winning the state championship for his school. Hadn't I once had the same dream? Too excited to think my idea through, I said, "How about meeting me here every night? We'll play one-on-one. I'll teach you every trick I know."

For the first time, Graham smiled. "You'd do that, T.J.?"

"On one condition." I stared deep into his eyes. "Don't ask me any more questions. Don't follow me, don't tell a single soul about me. It has to be a secret. If you bring some other kid with you, you'll never see me again. I swear it."

"Why?" Graham was puzzled, maybe even a little scared. I have that effect on people. I'm too intense, I guess, and it makes them nervous.

"It's none of your business why." This time I didn't care whether I offended him or not. It was important for him to take me seriously. "Promise. Cross your heart and hope to die."

Slowly, Graham put his hand on his chest. "Cross my heart," he whispered, "and hope to die if I ever tell a lie."

"Good." I got to my feet and stared down at him. "One other thing—we have to meet later than this. Someone could come along right now and see us." I was finally thinking straight. I'd been so happy to get my hands on a basketball I'd forgotten the rules. It was lucky I hadn't been caught.

Now Graham was really worried. "But I have a curfew." He glanced at his watch. "It's almost ten o'clock, and I was supposed to be home at nine thirty."

"Midnight," I told him, stepping deeper into the shadows, "or not at all."

"I'll have to sneak out," Graham said. "I could get in big trouble, T.J."

"Take it or leave it." I was backing away, keeping my eye on an approaching car, coming slow, its headlights pointed toward us, threatening to sweep across me.

The driver blew his horn. Graham stepped back on the curb and looked for me. "T.J.!" he yelled. "It's my dad. I have to go!"

From behind a tree, I watched Graham walk slowly to the car. His father yelled at him for staying out so late on a school night. Graham apologized and got into the front seat. As the car drove away, its headlights illuminated the empty playground.

Without Graham, the night seemed very quiet. In the distance, traffic rumbled on the interstate, a lonely sound reminding me of happy people with places to go and homes to return to.

Home. I had a home too — only I wasn't happy there.

The next night, long before midnight, I was under my tree, invisible in its shadow, watching and listening for Graham. Soon I heard him thudding across the asphalt, bouncing the ball as he ran. "T.J.," he called. "Where are you, T.J.?"

I loved the way his voice echoed, the way his shadow danced with him. "Here I am," I cried.

Graham whirled around, searching for me. I was right behind him, staying in his shadow, laughing. When he saw me, he sucked in his breath, amazed I was so close. "Where did you come from?"

Instead of answering, I grabbed the ball and darted across the court. He followed me, leaping to catch it on the rebound. We played till he collapsed on the asphalt, out of breath, sweaty, exhausted.

"I don't know how you do it," he said, his voice ragged.

Like before, I sat in the shadow. "I rest in the daytime," I told him.

"Me too, but I can't keep up with you."

I changed the subject then and got him to talk about his family. I wanted to hear all the details—his house, his bedroom, his brother and sister, his mother and father, his dog, what they ate for dinner, did they send out for pizza sometimes, did they go to the ocean or the mountains. I devoured everything he told me, especially the stories about his Irish setter. Next to basketball, the thing I missed most was my dog.

"But what about you, T.J.?" Graham asked. "What's your family like?"

That was the biggest danger of asking people too many questions. Sooner or later, they wanted to hear about you.

I scowled at him, but I had my answer ready. "We made a deal. No questions — remember?"

He mumbled an apology. "I forgot."

Getting to my feet, I said, "You'd better go home before somebody discovers you aren't in your bed."

"You'll be here tomorrow night?"

"At midnight."

I watched him race his shadow across the court. When he was out of sight but not out of earshot, I followed him down the dark streets, past houses sleeping on moonlit lawns, past cars reflecting streetlights in their windows, past cats gliding from bush to bush on feet as silent as mine. Crouching behind a tree, I saw Graham tiptoe up a driveway and let himself into a small brick rambler. He was home safe.

But not alone. Too quickly for him to notice, I slipped through the door behind him. The house was just as he'd described it, and I went from room to room, touching the things he'd told me about. Patty, the dog, raised her head and stared at me, but she didn't bark. A cat might arch its back and puff its tail and dance away sideways, but not a dog. Dogs know I mean no harm.

Before I left, I went to Graham's room and watched him sleep. I also peeked in on his little sister and his brother.

I lingered in his parents' room for a while, but his father snored so loudly it hurt my ears.

Still not ready to leave, I wandered into the living room and turned on the TV, not to watch it but to surprise the family in the morning. Graham's father would say, "Who turned on the TV?" and get cross when nobody confessed. For some reason, that amused me.

On my way out, I found the kitchen and stopped in front of a huge refrigerator. I opened the door and admired the food — sodas, milk, juice, eggs, butter, bread — enough stuff to feed all the kids at Graham's school.

In the freezer, I found a gallon of mint chocolate chip ice cream. I pressed it against my cheek and imagined how good it would taste, but I didn't eat any of it, not even a spoonful. I knew the rules.

From then on, Graham and I played basketball every night. Sometimes I followed him home; sometimes I went to other houses; sometimes I just roamed the streets. Depending on my mood, I climbed trees, borrowed bikes or skateboards, or swam in the community pool, gliding through the still water like a moonbeam. Every now and then, Patty came with me. I liked the sound of her paws on the cement, the feel of her warm breath on my hand.

As August slid into September, the nights cooled off. The crisp air smelled like dead leaves instead of honeysuckle. Graham began to improve, but just as he was becoming a real challenge, something happened that ruined everything.

We were sitting on the asphalt, taking a break. High above, the moon's full face peered down, no bigger than a dime but shining bright, casting more light than I realized.

Graham turned to me to say something and sucked his breath in. "T.J., you're, you're . . ." he whispered. "I can't believe I never noticed."

I backed away, too shocked to say a word. Graham had always struck me as the most unobservant boy I'd ever met. Now he was onto me, he'd discovered my true nature, and I was in big trouble.

He laughed. "It's okay, T.J. I don't mind playing basketball with a girl. I'm just surprised it took me so long to realize, that's all."

Limp with relief, I let my breath out in a long sigh. "Of course I'm a girl. I thought you knew."

Graham shook his head. "Do I feel dumb. It never occurred to me a girl could be named T.J. or play basketball like a pro. Plus, it's always dark when we meet. I haven't had a chance to get a good look at you." Moving closer, he reached for my baseball cap. "Take that off so I can see your face better."

"No." I was on my feet, running across the dark playground, leaping the wall that separated it from my home. The lawn was freshly mown. The gardener must have cut it while I was asleep. It smelled warm and sweet, the essence of last summer's sunshine.

"Wait, T.J.," Graham yelled. "Don't go."

I glanced back. He'd jumped the wall too. He was coming after me, shouting, pounding the ground with his heavy feet, breathing hard, making noise—so much noise. More than enough to wake the dead.

"I told you not to follow me!" I turned away from him and saw my parents waiting for me, their faces stern and pale.

"Dearly beloved daughter Theresa," Mom said sadly. "It appears you've broken the rules again."

"You'll be grounded fifty years for this," Dad said. "Perhaps you'll remember the rules the next time we let you out to play."

Aching with pain in the cold place that used to be my heart, I looked at Graham. He was frozen with fear, as rigid as the angel on the pedestal behind him. I took off my cap and showed him my face. It was a spiteful thing to do, but I was angry. Because of him, I would not see the stars or the moon for fifty long years. Watching him turn and run, I laughed. His scream was the last sound I'd hear till my punishment was over.

"Come, beloved Daughter." Dad took my arm and slowly, silently, like autumn leaves drifting down from trees, we laid ourselves to rest.

THE REAL THING

I walked down Third Street, peering into the windows of dingy antique stores, hoping to find what I needed among chipped plates, broken chairs, and eyeless teddy bears. In just a few days, Maple Hill would be celebrating its one hundredth anniversary with a parade down Main Street. If I wanted to ride on the float with the other Girl Scouts, I had to come up with a twenties-style dress. Most of my friends' mothers were making their outfits, but my mom couldn't sew a button on, let alone put together a whole dress. My friend Holly's mother offered to make one for me, but I decided to search the stores in the historic district instead. I wanted a genuine flapper dress, the real thing, with a dropped waist and lots of fringe.

I passed three or four shops but didn't see any old clothing in the windows until I came to All Our Yesterdays, a tiny place no wider than a hallway. In front of the open door was a rack of dresses, blouses, and other garments swaying gently in the summer breeze, price tags fluttering. I looked through them but found nothing resembling a flapper dress. Thinking there might be more clothes inside, I stepped cautiously into the shop.

At first I couldn't see a thing. Compared to the sunny sidewalk, the store was a dark pit, crammed with odd things. A stuffed polar bear towered over me, a stack of old magazines slithered across the floor, and Tiffany lamps hung from the ceiling, bumping my head as I ducked under them. Edging cautiously around a huge sideboard decorated with carvings of fierce animal heads, I made my way toward the rear of the store. So far I'd seen no clerk, but I heard old-fashioned music coming from somewhere in the back.

I finally found a saleswoman standing behind a counter. "Good morning, dear. May I help you find something?"

Her hair was white and she wore nice clothes, the kind my mother called "vintage classic," just right for an antique shop.

"I'm just looking," I told her.

"'Just looking'?" She waved an arm at the shop's contents. "Well, my dear, you could spend hours here, possibly days, 'just looking.' Why, I myself don't know what I've got in this place."

While she was talking, I saw a dress hanging on the

wall behind her. "That dress," I said. "The white one with the lace trim. It's just what I'm looking for."

She turned to see what I meant. "This one?"

"Yes."

She took the dress down and looked at it. "Well, now, I just said I don't know half of what I've got, and this dress proves it. I swear it wasn't here yesterday." She laughed. "At my age, your memory starts slipping, doesn't it?"

"I guess so." I touched the dress's soft fabric.

"Made of silk," she said almost to herself, "and trimmed with the finest Belgian lace."

While she talked, the old woman spread the dress on the countertop and smoothed it. "I must say, it would look lovely on you, my dear, just lovely."

"Do you think it will fit me?"

She eyed my figure. "Yes indeed," she said. "You can try it on, if you like." She pointed at a curtain strung across a doorway. "I use that closet as the fitting room."

Closing the curtain behind me, I yanked my T-shirt and jeans off and dropped the dress over my head. The light was a little dim, but I could see my reflection clearly enough to tell it fit perfectly. I leaned forward to admire the lace trim and noticed a brown stain and a small tear on the bodice.

I stepped out of the changing room. "How does it look?"

The woman smiled. "I knew it would fit. And it's so becoming. Why, you make a perfect flapper, my dear."

"But there's a stain." I pointed it out for her. "And look, the cloth is torn."

She put on her glasses and peered at the dress. "Why, yes," she murmured. "I'm sure it can be removed by soaking it overnight in a mild bleach solution."

"What about the tear though?"

"Oh, I can mend that easily enough." She smiled. "Bring it to me when you're dressed."

A few moments later, I watched her mend the dress with dainty stitches. "There," she said when she was finished. "As good as new. Except for the stain."

I smoothed the dress, loving the feel of it but worried about its price. Foolishly, I hadn't thought to ask. Now that it was mended, suppose I couldn't afford it?

"Considering the tear and the stain," the old woman said, answering my unspoken question, "I'll sell you the dress for five dollars. How does that sound?"

Sighing with relief, I counted out five of the twenty dollars Grandmother had given me for my birthday.

The old woman folded the dress carefully. After dropping it into a bag, she wrote a receipt and handed it to me. "You'll need this if you want to return the dress."

I looked at her name printed at the bottom of the receipt. "Thank you, Miss Ferguson," I said, "but I'm sure I'll keep it."

"Now that you know my name, will you tell me yours? The next time you visit, I'll feel like a friend has come to call."

"I'm Jenny O'Connor. I live on Bingham Road."

"Oh, yes, where the new houses are. In my day, that road didn't have a name. It was a dirt lane leading into town. My friends and I walked it many times. Nothing there then but fields and trees."

Miss Ferguson grabbed a cane and walked to the door with me. In the sunlight, her white hair shone like silver. "I don't want to sound nosy, but do you mind telling me why you want the dress?"

"It's for the anniversary celebration," I said. "Our Girl Scout troop has a float in the parade and we're all going to dress the way people did a hundred years ago."

"That was my mother's time, you know. She was a girl then, not much older than you are now." She smiled and touched my cheek with the tip of her finger. "You'll be the prettiest girl in the parade, wearing the prettiest dress."

"Thank you." I felt my cheeks redden with embarrassment. Holly was the prettiest girl in the troop, not me. "Well, goodbye," I added, "and thank you for sewing up the tear."

Hugging the dress to my chest, I hurried home to show it to Mom. Just wait till my friends saw it. They'd all wish they'd gone shopping on Third Street too.

Although Mom did her best to wash the stain away, she couldn't get rid of it. "Considering the age of the dress, the stain has had a long time to set," she said. "You'll have to cover it with something. A corsage, maybe."

I fingered the material. "It's beautiful, though, isn't it?"

Mom nodded. "You're lucky it fits so well. It's been a long time since I could get into a dress that size." Giving me a kiss, she added, "Run along to bed now, Jenny. It's late."

I hung the dress on the outside of my closet door and studied it, wishing I knew who'd worn it first. What was she like? Had she bought the dress for a special occasion? A dance, a party, a wedding? Before I fell asleep, I pictured a pretty flapper wearing my dress, foxtrotting around a ballroom floor in the arms of a tall handsome man.

I don't know what woke me, but when I opened my

eyes, the first thing I saw was the dress. Instead of hanging on the closet door, it floated slowly around the room as if it were dancing in the moonlight. At first I thought I was dreaming. Hadn't I been thinking about a ballroom full of dancers just before I fell asleep?

But this didn't feel like a dream. My room was my room, right down to the clutter of books on my desktop. My jeans and T-shirt lay on the floor where I'd left them. Cicadas buzzed outside my window. Traffic rushed by on the highway. A horn blew. A dog barked. Except for the dress, everything was ordinary, just the way it should be, not strange and distorted as it would be in a dream.

While I watched in horrified fascination, a girl slowly materialized inside the dress. I hoped I was dreaming, for if I was awake, I was face-to-face with a ghost. Pulling the sheet over my head, I lay still. The next time I opened my eyes, the ghost would be gone and the dress would be hanging on the door where I'd left it.

Nothing happened. No one moaned. No cold hand touched me. The dream was over, and the ghost was gone. Slowly I lowered the sheet. She was still there, a pale, motionless form at the foot of my bed.

"What do you want?" I whispered.

For a moment, she stared at me. Then, stepping back,

she raised her arm and gestured as if she wanted me to come with her.

"No," I whispered. "No."

The girl made no sound but beckoned once more. I shut my eyes and pulled the sheet over my face again, but it did no good. I felt her there, staring at me, beckoning. "No," I whispered through the sheet. "No. Please go away, please."

A whispery echo came back to me, no louder than warm summer air stirring the grass. "Please come . . . please."

I tried to call my parents, but as in a dream, I couldn't speak.

Slowly I lowered the sheet again. Surely she'd be gone . . . but instead, she'd moved closer, her face inches from mine.

"Please," she whispered again. "Please help me."

She stretched her hand toward me. When I drew back, afraid of her touch, she moved farther away, still beckoning, her eyes pleading.

I tried to look away from her but found it impossible. Drawn by a power I didn't understand, I got out of bed and followed her out of my room.

In the hall, the wood floor felt cool under my feet. I passed my parents' room, my brother's room. My father snored, but neither Mom nor David made a sound. "Wake up," I whispered to them. "Help me." But they didn't hear.

The living room was dark, the TV screen a gray blur. No one woke. No one stopped me. My dog didn't even bark. The girl opened the front door, and it closed behind me.

We crossed the lawn. The dewy grass chilled my bare feet and soaked the bottoms of my pajama pants. The moon was low in the sky, resting just above the Carters' garage roof. I glanced behind me at my house. Every window was dark. Inside, my family was sleeping peacefully. I longed to turn and run home, but the girl was just ahead, looking back at me, gesturing to me. She was on the road now. Her feet made no sound on the asphalt. I continued to follow her as if she led me on a string.

I hadn't gone far when I felt the paving turn to dust beneath my feet. The world around me shivered as if it were a reflection, agitated by a breeze on the water. My house and neighborhood dissolved into woods and fields.

I was truly frightened to see my familiar surroundings disappear. How was I to return to my home? Where was the girl taking me? What would happen to me when we got there?

I hung back, frightened to go on but unable to stop

myself from following her. She was farther ahead now and no longer alone. Three girls had joined her. Their voices drifted back to me, muffled by the trees arching over the narrow country road. They laughed and teased each other about the boys they might dance with or even kiss. Their dresses were in the same style—long waisted, knee length, some trimmed with lace, others with embroidery, some silk, some cotton. I heard the fabric rustle as they walked.

Shivering in the night air, I followed the girls down a path leading across a field. Ahead of us was an open-air dance pavilion ringed with old cars—Ford coupes, Model T's, and battered black farm trucks. It looked just like the pavilion in a photograph that hung in the library. Although it had burned down years ago, a bronze plaque marked the spot where it once stood.

I stared at the pavilion. What if I wasn't dreaming? What if I'd traveled back in time? The clothes, the old cars, the music coming from the dance floor all seemed right for the 1920s. Everything I saw appeared solid and real. I smelled the sweet odor of green grass crushed by automobile tires. I heard a baby crying, a man shouting, a woman laughing. It was as if I'd gone to a theater and somehow become part of the play.

A crowd of young people milled around me, girls in flapper dresses, boys in white shirts and slacks. No one noticed me, not even when I pushed and shoved my way through them. They were real and I wasn't. This was their world, not mine. But nothing explained why the girl had brought me here.

Despite the strangeness, I didn't feel I was in danger. Whatever happened, I wouldn't be harmed because I wasn't really here. I looked around, taking in the details of a night in the past, a night that had happened long ago.

Inside the pavilion, a band played and people whirled around the floor, dancing and laughing. I spotted the girl on the sidelines, talking to a tall handsome man. When the musicians paused before beginning a new song, the two of them joined the other couples. The girl's rosy face glowed with happiness.

Her friends watched her spin past. I moved closer to hear what they were saying.

"Who's that good-looking fellow Alice is with?" one whispered.

"I've never seen him before," another said, "but it seems he's swept her right off her feet."

"He'd sweep any girl off her feet. Me for instance." The first girl laughed.

"Uh-oh." The second girl grabbed her friend's arm. "Look who's coming. If Ben sees Alice with someone else . . ."

The three watched a young man—Ben—walk toward them. His face was red and sulky. "Who's that with Alice?" he asked.

One of the girls laughed. "Now, Ben, could it be you're jealous?"

Ben shoved his hands in his pockets. "It's no joke," he muttered. "Everyone knows I mean to marry Alice."

Over Ben's shoulder, I saw the stranger dance Alice through the crowd and out of the pavilion. Hand in hand, the two of them walked away from the lights and the music. Their shadows stretched across the grass toward the woods. Alice's pale dress fluttered in the breeze.

I hurried after them, determined to keep Alice in sight. She'd brought me here for a reason. I had to find out what it was.

On the edge of the woods, Alice stopped and turned to the stranger. I stood nearby and waited to see what happened next.

"Where are you taking me, Lawrence?" She smiled up at him.

He circled her waist with one arm and leaned close to kiss her cheek. "You're so lovely, Alice," he whispered. "I'd take you to the moon if I could."

Alice hesitated and looked back at the pavilion. "My friends will worry when they realize I've left the dance."

She took a step away as if she meant to return to the pavilion, but Lawrence seized her hands. "You're not afraid of me, are you?"

"Of course not." Alice laughed. "It's just that I'm practically engaged to Ben Perkins."

Lawrence kissed her again. "Ben's probably a nice fellow," he murmured, "but I doubt he's worthy of a girl like you."

Alice toyed with the long strand of beads she wore around her neck and let Lawrence kiss her.

"Come for a walk in the moonlight, Alice," Lawrence whispered. "What's the harm? Ben's at the pavilion. He doesn't know where you are."

The more I heard and saw, the more uneasy I became. Something was wrong. Perhaps Lawrence meant to harm Alice in some way. Did she expect me to protect her? How would I do that if I wasn't really here?

"Well," Alice said, "maybe we could take a little walk."

"We'll go back as soon as you like," Lawrence said. "Just say the word, and I'll return you to Ben Perkins." He gave Alice another kiss. "Just don't say it too soon."

Alice laughed and the two of them followed a path into the woods. I was right behind them.

"Don't go." I spoke as loudly as I could, but Alice didn't hear. "Don't go with him!" I clutched at her dress, but it melted away in my hands like moonlight. "Please, Alice," I cried. "Go back to the pavilion!"

I thought Lawrence heard my voice, for he looked at me, his eyes wide with surprise, but almost at once, I realized that it was Ben he saw, not me.

Before I fully understood what was happening, Ben yelled, "Get away from my girl!" and lunged at Lawrence, his fists raised.

Lawrence dodged a blow aimed at his face. When Ben came at him again, Lawrence raised his fists in defense. Alice begged them to stop, but for all the attention they paid to her, I might have been the one speaking.

As they jabbed at each other, ducking and bobbing in the moonlight, it was obvious that Lawrence knew more about boxing than Ben. Time and time again, he danced away from Ben's wild swings and landed his blows on

Ben's face and chest. Finally, Ben went down in the dirt, nose bleeding, eye blackening, shirt torn and bloody.

Lawrence stood over him. "Had enough?"

Alice grabbed Lawrence's arm as if she feared he'd hit Ben again. "You've hurt him."

Lawrence grimaced. "He started it, Alice. I was merely defending myself."

Turning to Ben, he stretched out his hand. "No hard feelings, pal. It was just a dance and a kiss on the cheek."

Ben got to his feet. He didn't shake Lawrence's hand. Instead, he pulled out a knife.

I saw it before the others did. "No," I cried, hurling myself at Ben. "No!"

He moved through me as if I were made of air and plunged the knife into Lawrence's heart.

Alice screamed and staggered back. "Ben!" she cried. "Ben, don't—"

In a fit of rage, Ben grabbed her and raised his knife.

I crouched down in the weeds and hid my face. I couldn't watch Ben kill Alice, but I couldn't leave. Alice wanted me to see her death. She wanted me to know who killed her. She'd brought me here not to save her but to be a witness.

From where I huddled, head down, afraid to move, I heard the unmistakable sound of Ben dragging the bodies off the field. He didn't take the time to bury them but ran deeper into the woods, crashing through bushes. Fallen branches snapped under his feet. Gradually, the noise faded, and I was alone.

I got to my feet slowly, fearfully, and looked around. In the spot where Lawrence and Alice died, the earth was stained with their blood. Ben had made a path through the weeds when he dragged Alice and Lawrence away. It disappeared at the edge of the woods.

What was I to do? I couldn't tell anyone at the pavilion what Ben had done. For one thing, no one could see or hear me. For another, the murders had taken place in the past. What happened next would happen as it had happened then.

I stared at the dark trees. Suppose the bodies had never been found? Could that be part of the reason Alice came to me? Not only because she wanted me to witness her death, but also because she wanted herself and Lawrence to be found and buried properly.

I looked at the woods. They were now part of the park, so it was possible the bones still lay where Ben had left them. But how would I find the bones after I returned to my time?

I stood in the moonlit field. The music from the pavilion stopped. People laughed and shouted good night to each other. Car doors slammed. Engines backfired. Horns blew. Not one of those people knew what I knew. Except Ben.

When everyone was gone, I walked slowly toward the dark pavilion. I knew where it was in my time, marked by the plaque. Perhaps I could find my way home from there.

When I walked past the building, I had the same sensation I'd had when I followed Alice, but stronger this time. The earth tilted under my feet, and trees swayed as if they'd come unrooted. The pavilion wobbled and suddenly spun away into the night.

To keep myself from falling, I grabbed a tree and pressed my face against its rough bark. Gradually, the spinning stopped, and I opened my eyes. I was standing on the plaque. Straight ahead was a fountain surrounded by flower beds and a circle of benches. I was back in my own time.

Never had I been so glad to see the path that led toward my house. Slowly, I began the long walk home. When I reached the corner, I looked down at my bare feet and my mud-stained pajama pants. If anyone saw me, I'd be mortified. But there seemed to be no danger of that. The road was deserted and all the shops were closed. According to the clock on the bank building, it was one thirty in the morning. I'd been gone for hours.

Frightened to be out so late, I ran home and sneaked in as quietly as I'd left. In my room, Alice's dress hung on the closet door, motionless in the moonlight. I buried my face in the soft fabric and grieved for the girl who once had owned it.

The next morning, I woke up early. It was Saturday and everyone was sleeping late. When I took the dress off the hanger, I noticed that the stain was darker than before—much darker. Worse yet, Miss Ferguson's careful stitches had come undone and the hole in the bodice was larger.

Carefully, I folded the dress and put it into a bag. Once again, I sneaked out without anyone seeing me and ran almost all the way to the shop. By the time I arrived, I was breathing hard. I saw through the glass door that the interior was dark. The hours were posted on a sign in the window: nine to five on weekdays, ten to four on Saturdays, and closed on Sundays. Across the street, the bank's clock said it was now eight forty-five. An hour and fifteen minutes to wait. My legs were shaky from running, so I sat on the sidewalk by the door and waited for Miss Ferguson to open the shop.

A little after nine, I saw her walking toward me. She carried a cup and a small paper bag in one hand and her cane in the other.

When she saw me, she cried, "Jenny, what on earth are you doing here? Are you all right? Has something happened?"

I stood up and pulled the dress out of the bag. "This belonged to a girl named Alice. She came to me last night and showed me how she died and who killed her."

Miss Ferguson put down her cup and bag and fumbled with her keys. "Come inside and tell me what you saw."

She brought me a bottle of water from a refrigerator in the back room and sat me on a stool behind the counter. Taking the other seat, she took a sip of her coffee, opened the bag, and offered me half of the bagel inside.

"Now," she said, "tell me everything."

By the time I finished, Miss Ferguson was crying. "Alice was my mother's best friend. She was with her at the dance when she left with Lawrence."

I gasped in surprise. "Your mother must have been in the group of girls I followed to the pavilion."

"Yes, I suppose she was," Miss Ferguson sighed. "Mother never forgot Alice. She spoke of her often — so often I know the story of her disappearance by heart."

"Was her body found? Was Ben tried for murder?"

Miss Ferguson shook her head. "Most folks assumed she'd run away with the handsome stranger, but Mother knew Alice wasn't the sort who would up and disappear without a word to her friends or parents. It pained her not to know what happened to her friend."

She blew her nose and wiped her eyes. "Mother always said something bad happened to Alice. She was convinced until the day she died that Ben had something to do with it. He had an awful temper and a jealous nature. I believed Mother."

Dust motes hung in the air between us. The store was so quiet I heard clocks ticking on a shelf behind me. "What happened to Ben?" I asked.

"According to Mother, he stayed in town for a month or so. He spent most of his time in a local tavern, brawling and drinking. After a while, he left Maple Hill and never returned. Nobody missed him, Mother said."

"What should we do?" I asked Miss Ferguson.

Looking me straight in the eye, she said, "Find the bones and make sure they have a proper burial. It's what she wants."

"But how will we do that? I don't remember where Ben left them."

"Wait here. I'll get someone to help us." Out the door she went, leaning on her cane but moving fast.

In a few minutes, she returned with a small spotted dog. "This is Lucy, a beagle born and bred to find things."

Lucy wagged her tail and offered me her paw. I shook it solemnly. "I'm Jenny," I told her.

The dog licked my nose and wagged her tail harder. Miss Ferguson smiled.

"You have a friend for life."

She showed the dog Alice's dress and made sure she sniffed the bloodstain. "You never can tell," she said. "There just might be a trace of something that will help Lucy find the bones."

Hanging a CLOSED sign in the shop window, Miss Ferguson locked the door, and we set out for the park. Everything looked so ordinary in the morning light. Two men played chess at a picnic table, a girl rode a scooter around and around the fountain while her mother watched from a bench. A group of boys had started a game on the ball field.

"Where should we begin?" Miss Ferguson asked.

"How about the plaque where the pavilion used to be?" I suggested. "Maybe something will look familiar to me."

But to my surprise, the field where Ben had murdered Alice and Lawrence was now part of the woods. Young trees had replaced the weeds I remembered from Alice's time. A narrow path wound through them in the general direction I remembered walking.

"That goes to the lake," Miss Ferguson said. "Fishermen use it."

Miss Ferguson released Lucy's leash, and the dog ran ahead, eager to sniff everything. The path wandered this way and that until I was so confused I wasn't sure of anything. In the woods, the trees had grown taller and thicker. Their roots invaded the path, making the ground lumpy under our feet. Miss Ferguson jabbed her cane fiercely into the earth to keep from stumbling.

I walked slowly, so Miss Ferguson could keep up with me. Every now and then, she swished her cane in the weeds or poked it into the underbrush. She whispered her mother's friend's name softly.

"Do you think Alice will lead us to the bones?" I asked.

Miss Ferguson whacked a bush. "If Alice could lead you into the past to witness her murder, surely she can help us find her bones."

Just then, Lucy began barking from somewhere up ahead of us. We left the path to find her, bending and stooping to avoid poison ivy and brambles. I tried to take Miss Ferguson's arm, but she said she was fine, she didn't need help.

We finally found Lucy in a thicket of honeysuckle and wild grapevine. She raised her head when she saw us and barked. Frightened of what we might see in the thicket, Miss Ferguson and I hesitated to go farther. Trees towered over our heads like silent witnesses. Leaves whispered. A bird called.

Miss Ferguson pushed ahead, leaning heavily on her cane. When she reached the dog, she made her way into the thicket and poked her cane into the tangled vines. The sun had found a gap in the foliage, and its light shone on Miss Ferguson's white hair.

She took off the scarf she wore around her neck and tied it to a branch to mark the spot. Snapping the leash on Lucy, Miss Ferguson walked back to me. "Do you want to come to the police station with me?"

"What will you tell them?"

"I'll say I was walking my dog and she found human bones in the woods. I'll tell them they might be the remains of my mother's dear friend Alice Watkins, who disappeared one hundred years ago. If real life is anything like movies and TV shows, they might identify Alice and Lawrence from cold case files and DNA."

I went to the station with Miss Ferguson to tell an officer about the bones. When she asked us if we were sure they weren't animal bones, Miss Ferguson said, "I know a human skull when I see one." A police officer was dispatched to the woods to find the site marked by Miss Ferguson's red scarf.

The discovery made headlines in the local newspaper. People who had heard stories about Alice wrote letters to the editor. The police began searching records they'd stashed in the basement years ago. A forensic specialist obtained DNA from the bones and tracked down relatives of Alice and Lawrence.

A month or so later, the remains were officially identified. Lawrence's relatives took him to his hometown. The church where Alice was baptized held a graveside memorial service and buried her in the Watkins family plot.

After the others left, Miss Ferguson and I lingered by the grave. Taking my hand, Miss Ferguson said, "We've experienced some very strange things since you came into my shop looking for a dress. You were so pleased to go home with the real thing."

"I'll never buy a used dress again." I shuddered at the memory of all I'd seen during my visit to the past.

Miss Ferguson hugged me. "But just think," she whispered, "if you hadn't bought that dress, no one would have known what happened to Alice. Her bones would still be lying there in the woods with Lawrence. You gave Alice peace, I'm sure of it."

While she spoke, a monarch butterfly hovered over Alice's grave and rested on her headstone for a moment.

"How beautiful," I murmured.

I watched the butterfly go to Miss Ferguson and sit on her shoulder. After a few seconds, the butterfly flew to me. Neither of us moved or spoke. Silently, scarcely breathing, I watched the butterfly leave us and fly high into the sky. It dwindled to a speck and vanished.

Miss Ferguson turned to me and spoke in a low voice.

"Did you know that many ancient cultures, the Greeks and the Irish for instance, believed butterflies are messengers from the dead? They come to tell us not to worry, not to grieve. They're at peace."

"Do you think Alice was here?" I stared at Miss Ferguson in awe.

Miss Ferguson sighed. "Who's to say for sure? But I like to think so."

Holding hands, we said goodbye to Alice and walked slowly away from her grave.

TROUBLE AFOOT

A while back, not more than a week or two ago, my parents gave me permission to visit my uncle Bert. He lived ten miles away in a small cottage — his "rural retreat," he fondly called it. Father and Mother agreed that a long walk in the fresh air would be beneficial to my health.

I set out on a sunny spring morning, anticipating a pleasant weekend in the company of my favorite relative. The previous day, I'd received a letter in which Uncle Bert mentioned finding something intriguing in a nearby lake. Since he and I shared an interest in marine biology, I was eager to learn more about his discovery.

Before I reached my destination, however, the weather changed abruptly. Clouds covered the sun. The wind rose and the temperature dropped. Rain fell in torrents. Thunder crashed overhead, and lightning shot to earth as if flung by Zeus's invisible hand. The storm raged like a gigantic creature bent on destruction, tearing limbs from trees and screaming in anger.

Soaked to the skin, I hurried onward, hoping to reach

my uncle's house before lightning struck me or rain drowned me. None too soon, I saw light shining from his window.

"Uncle Bert!" I cried. "Uncle Bert!"

Expecting to see my uncle's thin, bespectacled face peering out at me, I ran toward the cottage. He must have seen me coming. Why else would he leave the door wide-open on a night like this?

To my surprise, Uncle Bert did not appear, nor did he answer my calls.

When I reached the door, I stopped and stared in horror at the scene before me. The lantern hanging in the window swung wildly, casting moving shadows over broken furniture and scattered books and papers. Water puddled the floor, giving off the stench of rotten fish. Of my uncle himself, there was no sign.

In contrast to the storm, the cottage was silent. Still. Obviously empty.

Frightened, I stepped back into the rain. It was apparent that something dreadful had happened, but before I had a chance to seek help in the nearby village, a tree toppled to the ground, its massive trunk and branches blocking the road.

Thinking I'd be safer inside than out, I entered the cottage and shut the door. Despite the room's chaotic condition, a fire burned on the hearth, and a pot of stew simmered on the stove, reminding me I hadn't eaten since I'd stopped for lunch hours before. In addition to being hungry, I was cold, wet, and exhausted.

I moved closer to the fire and tried to come up with a logical explanation for the cottage's appearance. Perhaps Uncle Bert had been called away on business. He'd left in a hurry, neglecting to finish his meal and to close the door and windows. While he was gone, the storm struck, making it impossible for him to return. In his absence, the wind and rain rushed through the open door and windows, toppling furniture, scattering papers and books, flooding the floor.

Surely this scenario made more sense than vague conjectures of mayhem and murder. Shaking my head at my childish fears, I tidied the room as best I could, mopping up foul-smelling water, righting furniture, and stacking his books and papers in neat piles. Then, telling myself Uncle Bert wouldn't mind, I helped myself to the stew in the pot, which had no doubt been meant for me. When I'd eaten all I wanted, I made myself comfortable in a chair by the fire and waited for my uncle to come bounding through the door, laughing and apologizing for his absence.

Minutes passed, then hours, ticked and chimed by the old clock on the mantel. Outside, the storm continued to rage. I picked up a book, Charles Dickens's latest, but found myself reading the same sentences over and over again. Where was my uncle? When would he return?

Hoping to distract myself, I went to the table where I'd stacked my uncle's books and papers and began looking at them. Although I didn't recall Uncle Bert having an interest in such things, all of the books dealt with the same subject. Their pages showed evidence of frequent reading—marks and stains, notes in the margins, words underlined. Why would a marine biologist of my uncle's stature waste his time studying sea monsters?

I turned to his notebooks and leafed through them. Yes, there were the exquisitely drawn pen-and-ink sketches I remembered, the notes written in my uncle's careful hand, detailing the life cycles of mollusks and anemones, of crustaceans, of fish, both large and small.

But what was this? I stared, transfixed, at a drawing of what appeared to be an enormous prehistoric beast, something long since extinct, yet drawn with such vivid detail it seemed to spring to life before my very eyes. Pages of densely written notes accompanied the monstrous picture, not inscribed with my uncle's usual fastidious penmanship but hastily, even sloppily, scrawled across the page, almost impossible to read in the dim light of the fire.

Fetching the lantern from its hook, I bent over the notebook and struggled to decipher my uncle's words. Uncle Bert claimed to be writing a true account of his first sighting of the monster he'd drawn so carefully. Apparently he'd been caught in a storm near the lake. Taking shelter in the trees, he was astonished to see the head and neck of a huge serpent emerge from the water.

"The creature," he wrote, "appears to be of the same variety as the one believed to reside in Scotland's Loch Ness. Like the Scottish serpent, it has a long, slender neck and small head. I believe it to be over a hundred feet in length, dark brown in color, and covered with scales. Although it did not see me, it seemed to sense it was being watched and dove into the depths of the lake, leaving behind a noxious odor. At this point, I do not know if the creature is dangerous, but I intend to continue my observations."

I was tempted to shut the notebook and conclude that my uncle had lost his mind. Perhaps Uncle Bert's solitary existence had gradually weakened his reason, leaving him prey to the sort of nightmarish delusions I'd suffered in childhood — witches under my bed, monsters in shadowy corners, ogres creeping up the stairs to my room. Delusions I'd overcome, of course, as we all must if we are to retain our sanity.

Against my judgment, I went on reading, fascinated by Uncle Bert's growing madness. "A pattern is beginning to emerge," he wrote after several more sightings. "The creature surfaces only in rainy weather. Perhaps storms disturb its rest. I still do not know enough. I must go closer, perhaps draw its attention to myself, make contact with it somehow."

A few pages later, Uncle Bert's handwriting grew even more difficult to decipher. He seemed to be highly agitated, nervous, possibly frightened. A phrase here, a word there. "It's seen me . . . hostile, I fear . . . danger . . . must warn William, must . . ."

Then, on the notebook's last page, large wavering words ran across the wet paper: "Rain and wind tonight, rain and wind. Not safe here after all, not safe anywhere . . ."

My uncle had written nothing more.

I dropped the notebook and turned fearfully to the window. The storm had not lessened. The wind still blew fiercely, driving rain against the glass, breaking branches, toppling trees, howling like a beast circling the cottage. My childhood fears returned, seemingly strengthened by their long absence. At any moment, I expected the door to burst open, flung wide by a monstrous hand.

Despite my terror, I fell into a deep, if troubled, slumber near dawn. When I awoke, I gazed around the room, momentarily confused by the unfamiliar surroundings. Then, leaping to my feet, I ran to the door, nourishing the foolish hope that I'd see my uncle gathering firewood or engaged in some other morning routine. But he was nowhere in sight.

Nor was the storm over. Although its original fury had abated, rain fell steadily and the wind made a desolate sound in the trees. Grabbing Uncle Bert's oilskins from a hook by the door and donning them, I stepped outside. In the gray morning light, I simply could not believe that my uncle had seen a monster in the lake. However, he might have gone out into the storm looking for it. Perhaps he'd been trapped beneath a fallen tree. He might have lain outside all night, his cries swallowed up in the wind's roar.

Stricken with remorse for not having searched for him sooner, I followed a trail of uprooted trees, torn shrubbery, and gouged earth leading through the woods from the cottage to the lake. Only a cyclone could have cut such a wide swath of destruction, I thought, marveling at the power of nature.

"Uncle Bert," I called. "Uncle Bert, it's your nephew William. Where are you?"

Except for the wind and the rain, the woods were utterly silent. My voice echoed and reechoed, bouncing from tree to tree, now ahead, now behind.

A few moments later, I reached the lake, a vast expanse of dark water. I could not estimate its size. The far shore was shrouded in sheets of rain, giving the lake the boundless immensity of the sea itself. The wind drove waves before it.

I opened my mouth to call my uncle, but found I dared not make a sound. Except for the wind and the waves, the silence was as intense as the water was black.

Feeling as if I'd come to the edge of the known world, I stepped back and heard something crunch under my heel. At my feet, I saw my uncle's glasses. The lenses were broken, the frame twisted. His tweed cap lay a few inches away. A hiking boot in the style he fancied floated near the shore. Worst of all, I saw marks in the sand that could have been made by one thing and one thing only—a man's heels as he was dragged, still struggling, into the lake's dark depths.

At that moment, the lake's surface began to churn and the waves grew higher. Surf washed over my boots, the wind shrieked, and rain lashed my face like a stinging whip. Even though I had no wish to see what was causing the disturbance, I could not run. I might as well have been made of stone.

While I watched unwillingly, a narrow snakelike head, draped with sheets of foul-smelling algae and weeds, erupted from the waves. It turned its long neck and fixed its gaze on me. How long the creature stared at me I do not know, but I felt as if I was doomed to stand forever on the shore of that infernal lake, the object of a fearsome scrutiny.

Then, as suddenly as it appeared, the creature sank into the black water and vanished. Like a man released from a spell, I turned and ran, taking the path the monster itself had made as it pushed its way through the woods, seeking my poor uncle.

Bypassing the cottage, I followed the road until I came to the village. At the police station, the constable looked up from his papers, obviously startled by my appearance.

"What seems to be the trouble, young man?" he asked.

"The trouble is," I gasped, barely able to speak, "the trouble is . . . my uncle, Bert Pinkham, has disappeared."

"Bert Pinkham?" the constable echoed. "The chap who lives in Oak Cottage?"

"Yes," I whispered. "Last night, something . . . something . . ."

"Hold on a moment," the constable interrupted. "Start at the beginning, there's a good lad. Tell me what happened."

Trying to speak in a normal voice, I said, "When I arrived last night, the cottage was in disarray and my uncle was missing. This morning, I found some of his belongings beside the lake. I saw footprints, and then I saw . . . then I—"

Unable to go on, I burst into tears.

"I knew trouble was afoot last night," the constable said. "What with the storm and all. Sensed it coming, I did."

His voice trailed away as he fumbled with his pipe. "I warned your uncle not to meddle with it," he went on. "But he wouldn't listen. No, sir, the fool insisted on studying it. Spied on it. Drew pictures. Didn't give it a moment's peace."

I gazed at the constable, too frightened to defend dear old Uncle Bert. Clearly the man knew more about the thing in the lake than I did. No doubt he also knew exactly what end my poor uncle had met on that desolate shore.

"It likes its privacy," the constable added. "It don't care to be looked at; it don't care to be watched. If a cow or a sheep disappears, no one in these parts makes a fuss. We have the sense to let it be."

"But surely—" I began, only to be interrupted.

"Lord help you if it catches you looking at it," the constable cried, striking the desk with one fist.

Remembering the creature's dark and terrible stare, I began to tremble. "What do you mean, sir?" I whispered.

"Why, if it catches you looking at it, you're a goner," he said. "The creature won't rest till it tracks you down. No matter how far you run or how fast, lad, it'll find you."

Somehow, I got to my feet. Ignoring the constable's request to sit down and fill out some forms, I ran from his office.

Several weeks have passed since then. I have had no rest, no peace. I cannot sleep. I cannot sit down and enjoy a meal. I dare not return home for fear of endangering my poor parents. I run, walk, and stumble through towns and villages.

Always behind me, I hear a slithering sound, yet I do not look back. Clouds cover the moon, the wind rises, the rain begins. My nose burns with the stench of rotting fish; my skin is clammy. Oh, it would be better to be mad than to know, as I do, what follows me!

THE PUPPET'S PAYBACK

One rainy morning, Mom woke me, shaking my shoulder and shouting my name. "Jeremy, what are you doing in bed? You should be dressed and at the breakfast table. You've already gotten five demerits for tardiness from Miss Wockanfuss. Do you want to fail sixth grade?"

I shook my head. The only thing I really wanted was to pull the covers over my head and tell Mom I was sick, my throat hurt, my head hurt, my stomach hurt, I was getting a funny rash. But I'd tried all these symptoms already with no success. When your mother works, there's no way to stay home unless you're truly dying.

So I made my usual excuse. "The alarm didn't ring."

Of course, Mom didn't buy that. Without another word, she yanked my blankets off and stomped out of the room, leaving me cold and shivering and feeling sorrier for myself than usual.

Ten minutes later, I was sloshing through the cold rain toward school. While I was waiting to cross the street, a car sprayed me with muddy water. I jumped back from the curb and dropped my homework in a puddle. Naturally, I hadn't written it in indelible ink. When I fished it out, all my vocabulary words had dissolved into a blue blur. An hour's worth of work down the drain.

"Well, if it isn't Jeremy Germ."

Just ahead, Nelson Biggs blocked the sidewalk, holding out his hand, waiting for me to surrender my lunch money.

"Don't keep me waiting, Germ."

There was no use running, no use fighting. Wordlessly, I handed him a dollar bill. Instead of saying thanks, he punched me in the stomach.

"If they have spinach today," he said, "I'll give you mine."

When I got to school, I was one measly minute late, but Miss Wockanfuss got mad anyway, probably because she hated me and always had. You've heard of love at first sight. For Miss Wockanfuss and me, it was hate at first sight. "No excuses," she yelled. "In my classroom, punctuality counts!"

Miss Wockanfuss sent me into the storeroom to think about that.

After she let me out, she got angry all over again when she saw the soggy remains of my homework. "No excuses!" she hollered. "In my classroom, neatness counts."

Miss Wockanfuss sent me back to the storeroom to think about that.

In the cafeteria, I was the only kid who ate his spinach. As if that wasn't bad enough, Nelson jiggled my arm and made me spill half of it down the front of my shirt. For the rest of the day, I was known as "the green germ."

After lunch, Miss Wockanfuss caught me daydreaming. "No excuses!" she shouted. "In my classroom, paying attention counts!"

Back to the storeroom I went to think about that. The way things were going, I figured I'd spend the rest of my life in Miss Wockanfuss's storeroom.

Just before dismissal, Miss Wockanfuss caught me reading a library book when everyone else was doing long division. "No excuses!" she screamed. "In my classroom, reading doesn't count!"

This time, the storeroom wasn't enough. Miss Wockanfuss kept me after school. She made me write "I will be on time, I will be neat, I will pay attention, I will not read" 273 times multiplied by 99 and divided by 7.7.

She did not give back my library book, adding another

five cents to the quarter I already owed on it. Soon, the librarian would hate me too.

Hours later, I left school hungry, sad, and misunderstood. As I was passing a dark alley, I heard a funny, squeaky voice say, "Poor Jeremy Miller, oh, poor, poor Jeremy Miller—his day's been a killer!"

I stopped and peered into the shadows. "Who said that?"

A strange face popped up from behind a garbage can. It had beady little eyes, a long red nose, a wide mouth, and a big chin. It wore a jester's cap trimmed with bells. When it nodded its head, the bells jingled merrily. "Jeremy Germ, Jeremy Germ, you're an ugly worm."

Behind the garbage can was a shabby old man with the saddest face I ever saw. The puppet danced at the end of his arm. "Hello, sonny," the old man said softly. "How do you like Mr. Punkerino? I bet you never saw a finer puppet. Made of the best silk and satin and stuffed with pure glee."

The puppet laughed and clapped his hands. "Hooray, hooray," he crowed, "for Mr. Punkerino!"

"How did you know my name?" I asked. I wasn't sure

which of them to speak to, the puppet or the old man, so I looked between them. They were both staring at me.

"Name shame, who's to blame?" The puppet laughed louder, but the old man didn't even smile. Watching me closely, he reached out and moved the puppet nearer and nearer to me.

"I'm Mr. Punkerino," sang the puppet. "A jolly rogue am I! I'll make you laugh, I'll make you glad, I'll be the funniest friend you ever had!"

The old man held the puppet right under my nose. "Mr. Punkerino likes you, Jeremy," he said.

The puppet nodded his head, making the bells on his cap ring. "It would be grand if you'd give me a hand."

Suddenly I wanted that puppet more than anything in the whole world. I just had to have him. Without thinking, I reached for Mr. Punkerino. "Give him to me."

The moment the words left my mouth, a gust of wind sent dead leaves, old paper, and dirt spiraling toward me. In the middle of the whirling dust devil, everything turned dark. Then, as suddenly as it came, it was gone. I blinked and opened my eyes.

"Jeremy, Jeremy, now you must carry me."

The old man had vanished. I was amazed to see Mr.

Punkerino on my hand, grinning and waving his tiny fists. "You talked," I said. "You must be battery operated."

"Chattery, chattery," he said, "the best things are done without a battery."

The puppet was a tight fit, sort of like a glove a size too small, and he made my hand uncomfortably warm. I grasped his head, thinking I'd pull him off and figure out how he worked, but I couldn't budge him. It was as if he'd grown onto my hand. Even though it hurt, I yanked, tugged, and twisted till I was red in the face. While I struggled, the puppet shrieked, "Stop! Stop! I'll blow my top!"

Finally, I gave up and leaned against a wall. For a few seconds, the only sound was my breathing—and his. Yes, Mr. Punkerino was out of breath too. Worse yet, I could feel his heart beating like a trapped bird's.

Terrified, I stared into the puppet's beady eyes. "What are you?" I whispered.

A crafty grin spread across his face. "I can't say how," he said, "but I'm your pal now."

Suddenly a shadow fell across the alley's entrance. Hoping the old man had returned to explain the trick, I whirled around and saw Nelson Biggs glaring at me.

"Playing with dolls, Jeremy? I always knew you were a little strange."

Thrusting Mr. Punkerino behind me, I shook my head. I intended to run, but somehow my feet stayed where they were. "Get lost, you big fat dummy," I heard myself yell. "You're asking for a sock in the tummy."

Nelson stared at me in astonishment, but he wasn't any more surprised than I was. Even though the voice sounded exactly like mine, Mr. Punkerino had spoken, not me. I opened my mouth to explain. "Nelson, Nelson ate my lunch," I said instead. "Nelson, Nelson, want a punch?"

"Why, you little jerk." Nelson stepped toward me, his face purple with rage, but he never got a chance to hit me. Mr. Punkerino lowered his head, and my fist butted Nelson's stomach so hard it made my hand ache.

"Oof!" Nelson fell to the ground and stared at me, his eyes wide. "Have you gone nuts?"

"Crazy as a daisy," I said. "Loony as the moon."

Nelson backed away. At the end of the alley, he took one last wondering look at me and fled.

"Stinky, stinky Nelson," Mr. Punkerino shouted at my enemy's back.

"This is all wrong," I whispered to the puppet. "I'm supposed to make you talk, I'm supposed to make you move, but you, you—"

"Puppetry buppetry boo-hoo-hoo," Mr. Punkerino interrupted. "You've given your hand to a jolly old man."

Once more, I grabbed his head and yanked as hard as I could. The puppet fit tighter than before. I gave up in tears.

"There's nothing you can do," Mr. Punkerino said. "I'm really stuck on you."

Next, I tried to jam him into my pocket, but he beat me with his little fists and shrieked, "Take me home, take me home. Never will I roam!"

By the time I climbed the three flights of steps to our apartment, I was so exhausted I wanted to go to bed. Instead, I had to face my mother.

"You're late, Jeremy. Did Miss Wockanfuss keep you after school again?"

"She walked, she fussed, she even cussed," sang Mr. Punkerino. "I'm so bad I made her mad."

Mom stared at me. "What did you say?"

Before Mr. Punkerino could say more, I ran down the hall to my room. "I have to do my homework!" I yelled and slammed the door.

When it was time for dinner, I kept Mr. Punkerino in my lap and tried to eat with my left hand. Mom looked at me with a puzzled expression. "Is something wrong, Jeremy?"

I shook my head. If I didn't open my mouth, maybe Mr. Punkerino couldn't speak. Of course, I underestimated him. Peering over the edge of the table, he waved his little fists at Mom.

Mom stared at Mr. Punkerino. "Where did you get that dirty old puppet, Jeremy?"

Mr. Punkerino scowled. "I'm cleaner than you. You smell like a shoe."

"Don't be impudent," Mom said to me. "Take that thing off your hand and eat your dinner." Impatiently she reached out to grab the puppet, but he dodged aside.

"I'm sorry," I said desperately. "We're putting on a play at school. Miss Wockanfuss told us to wear our puppets all day. That way we'll get used to them, they'll feel natural on our hands, they'll seem like they're part of us."

Mr. Punkerino laughed. "Give a puppet a hand," he sang. "You'll soon understand!"

Mom smiled. "You should get an A the way you bring that puppet to life. I swear his face changes, his eyes twinkle. Why, he all but breathes."

•••

The next morning, I left for school an hour early, hoping to find the old man in the alley and make him take the puppet back. Miss Wockanfuss already hated me. What she'd do when she saw Mr. Punkerino didn't bear thinking about.

At the entrance to the alley, Mr. Punkerino said, "You can't give me away. I'm yours for many a day."

I ignored him.

The old man was going through the trashcans, making so much noise he didn't see me until I was close enough to grab his sleeve.

"No," he whispered. "No, not you."

I didn't know whether he meant me or Mr. Punkerino, but I thrust the puppet at him. "You put this on my hand. Now take it off!"

"Fickle, fickle," Mr. Punkerino said, "got a face like a pickle."

The old man shook his head. "Begging your pardon, but nobody can give you what you don't want. You asked for him. You got him."

Before I could say a word, the old man pulled loose and ran, a flash of gray rags disappearing down the alley. By the time I reached Elm Street, there was no sign of him.

It looked like I'd have to take Mr. Punkerino to school after all. If he acted up—and I was sure he would—I'd probably spend the rest of my life in the principal's office.

I slid into my seat just as the bell rang. Miss Wockanfuss shot me a nasty look, but she couldn't send me to the storeroom. For once, I wasn't late.

Mr. Punkerino behaved for a while. He stayed on my lap, out of sight. Every now and then, he sighed, but he didn't speak. Then a folded piece of paper landed at my feet. A note to pass on, I thought. But no—it had my name on it. I opened it cautiously, thinking it might be a death threat from Nelson.

"I hear you socked Nelson Biggs," I read. "I think you're wonderful." It was signed "Violet Rose."

I glanced at her, and she smiled so sweetly my heart stopped for a second and then beat so fast I thought it would fly out the window. Violet Rose had never even looked at me before. Could this mean she liked me?

"Jeremy!" Miss Wockanfuss thundered. Her bosom swelled, her face turned red. She strode down the aisle, shaking the floor like a brontosaurus on a rampage. "Why are you smiling? No excuses! Happiness is not allowed. Nobody has a good time in my class!"

She was just about to send me to the storeroom to think about that when Mr. Punkerino said, "Walk and fuss, walk and cuss. You look like a junkyard bus."

For a moment, there was deadly silence. My classmates held their breath; they didn't move; they didn't even blink. Miss Wockanfuss puffed up like a balloon about to explode.

"Jeremy Miller, you go to the principal this moment!" she shouted.

When I stood up to leave, Mr. Punkerino shook his fists and laughed. "You make me ill, you big fat pill."

Violet Rose turned pale. Nelson gasped. The whole class cowered.

Miss Wockanfuss reached for Mr. Punkerino. "Give me that!"

In a flash, the puppet was on Miss Wockanfuss's hand. She stared at Mr. Punkerino, looking shocked. At that moment, the principal entered the room.

"Miss Wockanfuss," Mr. Dinkerhoff said, "what's going on in here? I can hear the noise in my office all the way down the hall."

Miss Wockanfuss was struggling to remove the puppet, but her efforts didn't stop Mr. Punkerino from saying, "What's it to you, Mr. Dinkydoodoo?"

It was Mr. Dinkerhoff's turn to be outraged. "What did you say?"

Miss Wockanfuss shook her fist, her face purple, but she couldn't free her hand or silence Mr. Punkerino. "I've had it with you, Mr. Dinkydoodoo," he sang. "Go jump in a lake, you silly old fake!"

Mr. Dinkerhoff took Miss Wockanfuss by the arm. Turning to us, he said, "Please excuse your teacher's behavior, boys and girls. She isn't well."

"Quick, quick, I'm sick, I'm sick," cried Mr. Punkerino. "Take me away. Call it a day!"

"Yes, yes, dear Emma," Mr. Dinkerhoff said soothingly. "Sit tight, boys and girls. We'll send a substitute as soon as we can."

Still shaking her fist, Miss Wockanfuss left the room. Just before he disappeared with her, Mr. Punkerino waved to me. "So long, goodbye, please don't cry. You won't see me again. I've found a new friend."

For a few moments, nobody spoke. Then Violet Rose got to her feet. "Hip hip hooray for Jeremy," she shouted. "Let's give him a great big hand for getting rid of the meanest teacher in the world!"

Everyone clapped, even Nelson.

I'd like to say I felt sorry for Miss Wockanfuss, but even

when they took her away in a straitjacket, I felt sympathy only for Mr. Punkerino. Poor puppet—he didn't know what a bad hand he'd been dealt.

THE NEW GIRL

Madeleine had never gone to any school but Miss Ida's Private Academy for Girls. But for reasons she didn't understand, Mama and Papa had brought her to a school very different from the academy. Built of dark stone, the building loomed above her, its narrow windows almost hidden by the ivy climbing the walls. Tall, drooping trees surrounded it. Their leaves dripped as if invisible rain fell, dampening the moss and ferns that flourished everywhere.

Madeleine looked at her parents. "Surely you aren't leaving me here," she whispered. "I don't like this place. I'm scared."

Mama and Papa kissed her and cried. They told her how much they loved her; they said they hated to leave her, but it was clear she had to stay here—she could not go with them.

In disbelief, Madeleine watched them walk away, their heads bowed in sorrow.

"Mama," she called. "Papa, wait! Take me home with you. I beg you!"

But they neither answered nor looked back. It was as if she hadn't spoken.

In desperation, Madeleine ran after them, but her legs were too weak to catch up. Well ahead of her, they passed through a tall gate. With a clang, it swung shut behind them. Murmuring to each other, they disappeared into a dense fog.

"Come back," she cried. "Come back!"

No one answered, but she heard the sound of a horse pulling a carriage away. She knew Mama and Papa were in that carriage. They were leaving her.

Madeleine sobbed and seized the gate's handle with both hands and pulled. The gate didn't budge. She pulled harder, she shook it, but the cold iron hurt her hands, and she had to let go.

Her parents were gone. The sound of the carriage was gone. She heard nothing but the call of mourning doves from somewhere behind her. For reasons she didn't understand, her parents had deserted her.

Sinking down on a stone bench near the gate, she waited. If her parents loved her, they would return.

"You must be Madeleine, the new girl."

Startled, Madeleine looked up. Although she hadn't heard him approach, a boy stood in front of her. Perhaps a year or two older than herself, he had a long, melancholy face. Dressed as if for a formal occasion, he wore a black jacket and pants, a white shirt with a tall, stiff collar, and dark shoes polished to a shine. Rather old-fashioned clothing, Madeleine thought, but quite respectable. She glanced down at her blue silk dress and hoped it was suitable.

"Please forgive me for keeping you waiting," he said. "I should have been here to greet you when you arrived. My name is Alfred, and I am to be your escort."

Madeleine turned her head to wipe her eyes. She didn't want the boy to think her a crybaby.

Alfred held out his arm as if he meant her to take it and walk with him.

"Thank you, Alfred." Remembering her manners, Madeleine rose to her feet and placed her hand in the crook of his elbow. For a moment, she was tempted to giggle at the picture they must make—he in his out-of-date formal clothing and she in her silk dress, the most fashionable style among her friends.

"By the way," he said softly, "it's perfectly acceptable to be sad, even to weep. We are all unhappy when we arrive. And often confused."

"I am indeed unhappy and confused. My parents left me without any explanation. They cannot mean for me to remain." Madeleine shuddered. "It's cold and damp and miserable. The very air tastes of sorrow."

Alfred patted her hand. "I understand. I once felt the same way. You'll get used to it after a while and it won't seem so bad."

Madeleine didn't answer, but she was certain she'd never get used to this place. Soon Mama and Papa would fetch her, and they'd go home and she'd sleep in her own bed.

In front of the school, Madeleine looked up the steep steps at the dark door and felt sick. She wasn't the sort of girl who fainted, but she felt as if she might become one.

The school door opened and a tall woman peered down at them. She was pale and thin. Most likely she was Alfred's mother, Madeleine thought.

"You're quite late," the woman said. "I was beginning to fear there was a problem."

"It was Benjamin. He wanted to—"

"No need to say more, Alfred." Turning to Madeleine, she said, "I am Miss Simpson, your instructor. Please come up, dear. I'm eager to meet you."

With Alfred steadying her, Madeleine climbed the

steps slowly. At the top, she was out of breath. She was still weak from the pneumonia that had kept her in bed so long.

"Oh my, what a pretty girl you are." Miss Simpson leaned down and kissed Madeleine on the cheek. Her lips were cold and dry. Madeline forced herself not to draw back from the kiss.

"And your dress, so well cut and such a lovely shade of blue. Is it the fashion now?"

"Thank you," Madeleine said. "Mama had Miss Jones make it for me from a Paris pattern. I wore it to Sylvia Long's birthday party — her twelfth. I'm soon to be twelve myself. Mother has already ordered another dress for me in the prettiest shade of pink. I'll wear it to my party."

"How lovely," Miss Simpson said, but Madeleine saw her glance at Alfred and shake her head ever so slightly, as if having a new dress wasn't lovely at all.

"Forgive me. I hope you don't think I'm putting on airs," Madeleine said. "I'm excited about my party. I've been very ill, you see, and I feared I wouldn't recover in time for my birthday."

"No, no, of course I didn't think such a thing of you, my dear." Miss Simpson took Madeleine's hand and led her into a vestibule that seemed as cold and damp as the air outside. It smelled old and dusty, like the basement in her house. Someone should open the window and let fresh air inside, she thought.

Alfred followed them down a long hall. Madeleine was relieved that he'd released her hand. She'd begun to fear he thought she needed his support. She'd needed help when she was sick, but now that she'd recovered, she was proud to walk on her own two feet.

Miss Simpson stopped at an open doorway and said, "Here is your classroom."

Madeleine counted five students—three boys ranging in age from six to ten, she guessed, and two girls, one about her age and the other a few years younger.

Judging by the size of the building, Madeleine had expected a classroom for each grade.

Miss Simpson must have noticed her surprise. "It's only January," she said. "We'll have more students as the year progresses." She looked sad as she said this.

"I don't understand," Madeleine said.

"They come when they're ready. You'll see." Turning to the children, Miss Simpson introduced them. "Richie is our youngest—only five, poor little lamb. John is seven, and Paul is eight. Alice is eleven like you, and Jane turned thirteen just before she joined us. Benjamin is absent, but he'll be back with us soon."

Turning from Madeleine to the students, she said, "Say hello to Madeleine, boys and girls."

Madeleine smiled and nodded as they greeted her. Since she was certain to be leaving soon, she made no effort to remember their names.

"Now, Madeleine," Miss Simpson continued. "You needn't stay for today's lesson. I'm certain you're tired and need to rest. Alfred will show you the sleeping quarters. You may remain there until you hear the bell chime at six o'clock."

Relieved to escape the stares of her new classmates, Madeleine followed Alfred down a long hall and up a staircase to the second story.

As they rested at the top of the steps, Madeleine asked, "Why is it so dark inside this building? And cold? I'm shivering."

"It's the climate. Mist and fog block the sunlight year round," Alfred told her. "You'll get used to it. Everyone does."

He took her hand again, and they walked down another long, dim hall. Madeleine expected their footsteps to echo on the hardwood floor, but silence filled her ears as if they were stuffed with balls of cotton.

"I don't wish to be rude," Madeleine said, "but this is a very strange place. I don't like it. When will Mama and Papa take me home?"

"This is your home now," Alfred said.

"No!" Madeleine stamped her foot in frustration. "I live on Grant Street with Mama and Papa and my sister and brother. I don't know why I'm here, but soon I'll go home."

Alfred looked at her sadly. "I thought you understood, Madeleine."

"Take me back to the gate. I'll wait for Mama and Papa there."

"You must stay here and do what you're told."

Madeleine broke away from Alfred and ran down the stairs, down the hall, past the classroom, and out the front door. The fog was so thick now she barely found her way to the gate. Grabbing the handle, she pulled with all her might, but the gate refused to budge. Once again, the cold metal hurt her hands, and she was forced to let go.

The fog on the other side was thicker than it was on her

side. If she hadn't seen her parents walk into that dense gray wall, she'd think nothing existed beyond the gate.

"Mama, Papa," she cried. "Come back!"

Alfred put his hand on her shoulder. "They can't hear you, Madeleine."

Although his touch was gentle, Madeleine recoiled as if a snake had bitten her. "Why does everyone insist on keeping me here? My birthday is next week. I have to be there for my party." She tried not to cry, but she couldn't fight her tears. "Am I being punished? Is that it? Must I stay here until I repent for something I don't remember doing?"

"No, no, of course you're not being punished."

"Then why did Mama and Papa leave me in this horrid place? Why can't I go home?" She paused a moment. "They don't love me anymore, do they? They want to be rid of me."

"Believe me," Alfred said, "they love you very much. It was very painful for them to leave you."

"Painful for them? What about me?"

Alfred shook his head. "Come away from the gate. It does you no good to linger here."

Too tired to resist, Madeleine allowed Alfred to lead

her back to the school. As they passed Miss Simpson's door, she saw the teacher welcoming a boy about her age to the classroom. Although she got no more than a glimpse of him, he seemed to be as unhappy as she was.

Up the stairs and down the hall again, but this time Madeleine was too exhausted to break away from Alfred. She'd been sick so long, it was no wonder she tired easily.

Alfred ushered her into a large room lined on both sides with small beds, made up with white sheets and pillows.

"Where are the children who sleep in these beds?" Madeleine asked.

"They will arrive as time passes. Remember what Miss Simpson told you. The year has just begun."

"I don't understand." Madeleine yawned. She was so tired.

Alfred stopped about halfway down the row of beds. "This is where you'll sleep. Rest, but don't forget to come downstairs when you hear the dinner chime."

The bed was hard and narrow. Madeleine lay on her back and closed her eyes. Sleep, she thought, yes—her body needed sleep. Perhaps it was a rest home or a convalescent hospital, and she was meant to stay here until she'd fully recovered from pneumonia.

Perhaps she hadn't heard Papa tell her why she was here. While she'd been sick, she'd had trouble understanding what people said. Mumble, mumble, mumble, and someone crying, that's all she'd heard.

Just as she thought she might fall asleep, she saw a boy enter the room. He was accompanied by an older girl who was explaining things to him. Madeleine supposed the girl was his escort.

Through half-closed eyes, she watched the boy lie down on the bed beside hers. That was strange. Shouldn't the boys have a separate room?

Madeleine sat up and called to the girl who had already turned away. She stopped and looked at Madeleine. "May I help you with something?"

Madeleine beckoned her closer and whispered, "You've left that boy in the wrong place. This room is for girls."

The girl smiled at her. "Things like that don't matter here. Boys or girls, you're all children to us."

"I don't think my parents would approve."

"Please don't worry. It's of no concern." Before Madeleine had a chance to protest, the girl walked away.

The boy looked at her shyly. "My name is Benjamin," he said. "This is the worst school I've ever seen. I want to go home, but no matter how often I try to escape, someone catches me and brings me back. It was Alfred last time. He's the biggest one here."

"I'm Madeleine." She smiled at him. He seemed to be a nice boy, very pale, wearing a well-pressed shirt, black jacket, black knee pants, and long black stockings. His Sunday best, she thought, except for one thing.

"Where are your shoes?"

Benjamin looked down, apparently surprised not to see his shoes. "I don't know. Perhaps they were muddy, and I left them at the door."

Perhaps he had. Boys were notoriously careless with their belongings. Why, just since Thanksgiving, her brother had lost three pairs of mittens and a scarf Mama had knitted for him.

"Where do you live, Benjamin?"

"Number Fifteen Forest Drive."

"I live at Number Five Grant Street, near the park."

"What school do you go to?" Benjamin asked.

"Saint Timothy's. The nuns are scary, but I have lots of friends. I'm a champion jump-roper."

"I go to Henry Ford Public School. I'm on the softball team. I hit five home runs last year. This year, I'll break the record."

They sat side by side on Benjamin's bed. "I hope they let us go home soon," he said.

"Me too." Madeleine sighed. "Were you sick before you came?"

"I had a very bad case of whooping cough."

Madeleine nodded. "I think we've been sent here to recover. I'm still very weak, but as soon as I'm stronger, they'll send me home."

Benjamin smiled. "Yes, you're probably right. I noticed that the children in the classroom all looked thin and pale."

"If we go home in time, will you come to my birthday party?"

"Sure," Benjamin said, "as long as you don't play spin the bottle. I hate kissing games."

"I hate them too." They smiled at each other. "Now we have something to look forward to."

When the chime rang, Madeleine and Benjamin went to the top of the steps. Below them, the children left the classroom and walked down the hall.

"I guess we should follow them," Benjamin said.

"It's suppertime," Madeleine said, "though I must say I'm not hungry."

"I'm not either. My throat was sore for so long, I ate nothing but gelatin and ice cubes."

"Ice cubes aren't food."

"They seemed like food."

When they reached the bottom step, they saw the other children entering a room at the end of the hall. Miss Simpson appeared in the doorway and beckoned to them. "Madeleine and Benjamin, come along."

The children sat at a long table set for a meal. Plates, glasses, and silverware all were placed in the proper order. A folded napkin lay at each place. Madeleine observed many more places than children. Indeed, rows of empty tables were also set for dinner even though no one sat in the chairs.

She and Benjamin looked at each other with raised eyebrows. Madeleine turned to the girl next to her. Was she Alice or Jane? Madeleine couldn't remember.

"Why are so many places set?" she whispered. "Are more children coming?"

Jane or Alice, whoever she was, shook her head and pressed a finger to her lips. Apparently, the children were not allowed to talk at meals.

Miss Simpson stood at the head of the table. "Roast

beef and mashed potatoes tonight," she said. "You may begin."

To Madeleine's amazement, the others lifted their forks and ate from empty plates. They drank from empty glasses. They buttered invisible bread and nibbled it daintily, wiping their fingers on their napkins.

"What are they doing?" Benjamin whispered to Madeleine.

"They must be practicing their manners. We'll have real food later."

Miss Simpson directed her attention to Madeleine and Benjamin. "You're not eating," she said. "Aren't you hungry?"

Madeleine went along with the game. She picked up her knife and fork and pretended to cut slices of roast beef. Beside her, Benjamin watched the others eat and drink and butter their bread.

"Benjamin," Miss Simpson said. "Your dinner is getting cold."

"Please, miss, how can I eat if there's nothing on my plate?" Benjamin spoke softly but he did not falter, nor did he look away from Miss Simpson.

Madeleine held her breath and waited for Miss

Simpson to answer. The other children did not look at anyone. Keeping their heads bowed over their plates, they continued to eat what wasn't there.

Miss Simpson leaned across the table. "Jane, please tell Benjamin how good the beef is tonight."

Jane looked at Benjamin. "It's delicious—cooked just right and very tender. The mashed potatoes are drowning in gravy. They melt in your mouth."

Richie smacked his lips. "I've already eaten everything on my plate."

"Me too." John held up his plate. "May I have another helping?"

While Miss Simpson spooned invisible food onto John's plate, Madeleine nudged Benjamin. "Just pretend to eat. Like this." She raised her fork and swallowed a mouthful of imaginary mashed potatoes. "Yum yum. The best I ever ate."

Miss Simpson smiled and nodded her head. *If I'm a good girl, perhaps I'll be sent home soon,* Madeleine thought.

"We're having blueberry pie with ice cream for dessert," Miss Simpson announced. "Unfortunately, children who refuse to eat dinner will not get dessert."

Benjamin's face turned red and his eyes filled with tears. "I want to go home. Right now!" He pushed his chair back from the table, but the girl who'd brought him to Madeleine's room suddenly appeared and made him sit down.

"You may not leave the table until you eat your dinner," she told him.

"But I have no dinner to eat!" Benjamin held his plate upside down. "See? And look at this." He turned his glass over. "There's no food and no milk."

The other children began to murmur to each other. Madeleine said nothing but waited to see how long the game would last. If there were winners and losers, Benjamin was definitely not a winner.

"Sheila," Miss Simpson said, "please take Benjamin upstairs and put him to bed. I cannot allow him to disrupt our routine."

"Madeleine," Benjamin cried. "Turn your plate and glass upside down. Show them."

But Madeleine lowered her head and pretended to cut another piece of beef. Benjamin didn't understand, but she did. She knew how to play games.

Sheila dragged Benjamin out of the room and up the stairs. His shouts faded, and silence dropped upon them like a soft gray cloud.

With a troubled face, Richie turned to Miss Simpson.

"Why was Benjamin's plate empty? My plate wasn't empty, was it? I ate my roast beef. Or was it chicken?"

"Of course you ate your dinner. We had roast beef tonight, your favorite." She paused and gave Richie a long, sad look. "Benjamin is new here. The first night can be difficult, especially for some children."

The children murmured and nodded, but Richie looked at his plate uneasily.

Miss Simpson beamed at Madeleine. "Our new girl did very well, very well indeed. As a reward, Madeleine shall have two scoops of ice cream with her pie."

Madeleine looked modestly at her empty plate. She didn't mind pretending she'd eaten. She wasn't hungry anyway. When the game was over, perhaps she'd have an appetite.

Miss Simpson rang a small silver bell, and a very old man entered the room. Madeleine watched him collect the unused plates and silverware. He was wrinkled and thin and barely more than a skeleton with wisps of white hair on his head. His back was so badly bent that his head stuck out like a turtle's poking out from a shell. As he took Madeleine's plate, she shifted away from his bony fingers, fearing she'd scream if he touched her. He smelled bad, and his clothes were old and dirty. If Madeleine had been hungry, the sight of the old man would have taken her appetite away.

After he'd cleared the table, he returned pushing a wobbly little cart with squeaky wheels. He gave each child an empty plate. They waited politely, hands folded in their laps, and did not begin to eat their dessert until everyone was served.

Under Miss Simpson's watchful eye, Madeleine joined the rest of the children in their strange game. "Blueberry pie is my tip-top favorite," she said. Like the others, she wiped her mouth and fingers with her napkin and then laid it neatly folded beside her dessert plate.

After dinner, Miss Simpson led the children down a shadowy wood-paneled corridor to a pleasant room furnished with sofas and chairs. Madeleine saw books and games and puzzles lying on low tables. A piano stood in one corner.

After the children were seated, Miss Simpson asked Alice to play the piano. "Perhaps Chopin's Prelude in E Minor, opus 28, number 4," she suggested. "Such a lovely, somber melody. It gives me shivers to listen to it."

Madeleine had taken piano lessons for four years.

She'd mastered that particular prelude not long before she fell ill. She perched on the edge of a sofa, eager to hear it again.

Alice raised her hands over the keyboard. Madeleine took a deep breath and waited for the music to begin. The etude's melancholy suited the setting, she thought, the darkness inside and out, the heavy mist, the sorrow.

Alice's hands touched the keys. She showed every sign of playing, but there was no sound. Madeleine looked around the room. The others seemed entranced. Paul gently nodded his head as if in time with the music. Miss Simpson smiled and gazed into the distance as if the etude summoned images of a memory dear to her. Jane closed her eyes and moved her fingers as if she herself were sitting at the piano. It seemed to Madeleine that everyone heard Chopin's music. Everyone, that is, except her.

When Miss Simpson glanced at her, Madeleine nodded as if she heard what the others heard. Another game— goodness, how many games must she play before she was allowed to go home? The acting was growing tiresome.

Alice struck the final chord, and everyone clapped. Miss Simpson told her she'd never played the etude better. Alice curtsied.

The children broke into small groups, some to read,

some to do puzzles, some to play games. Jane challenged Madeleine to dominoes. Madeleine picked one tile up, but it was blank. She turned over another and another and another—all blank.

She looked at Jane and saw that she was laying out a line of dominoes as if she were matching the dots. They were all blank.

"Well?" Jane asked. "Don't you know how to play?"

Madeline shook her head and pushed her dominoes toward Jane. "Sorry. I guess I've forgotten."

Jane called to Alice and the two of them began to play. More pretend. Madeleine's brain was tired. She picked up a book but when she opened it, the pages were blank.

Near her, John appeared to be reading.

"Is that a good story?" she asked.

He held it up as if to show her the cover, which was plain blue. "*Treasure Island*. Have you read it?"

"Yes, of course. It's one of my favorites. Can I see it?"

John handed her the book. "Don't lose my place."

Unsurprisingly, its pages were also blank. Madeleine gave it back and went to the puzzle table. Paul and Richie were working on a jigsaw. All the pieces were white.

"What will that be when you finish?" Madeleine asked.

Paul showed her the lid of a white box. "It's a herd of

horses galloping across a field. I love the black one. See? I think he's the leader. Just look at the way he holds up his head and arches his neck. You can see his teeth and the whites of his eyes."

Richie pointed at the puzzle. "Paul found all the corners, and, look, we've got some of the horses—a head here, a tail there."

"Do you like puzzles?" Paul asked. "You can help if you want."

Madeleine shook her head. "No, thank you. I'm too tired to pretend."

"Pretend?" Paul stared at her. "What do you mean?"

Miss Simpson touched Madeleine's shoulder, and Madeleine jumped. She hadn't realized the teacher was beside her.

"Perhaps you should be in bed, dear. You must be very tired."

"Yes, ma'am," Madeleine said. "I'm so very, very tired." She yawned for emphasis.

Alfred appeared as if he'd been waiting just outside the door.

"Please take Madeleine upstairs," Miss Simpson said. "I've been watching her. The poor child is still having difficulties."

"I'm not having difficulties," Madeleine said. "I'm pretending as hard as I can. Isn't that what you want?"

"You shouldn't need to pretend, dear. It indicates you're not ready for the next step."

"Do you mean going home? Is that the next step?"

"Please go with Alfred. The others must not be upset twice in one night."

Alfred took Madeleine's arm, and she allowed him to lead her out of the room and down the long dark hall.

At the bottom of the staircase, Madeleine stopped. "Please, Alfred, tell me why nothing is real here."

"What do you mean?"

"You must have noticed. Everything is pretend. At dinner, the children eat imaginary food. In the room we just left, Alice plays the piano and everyone but me hears Chopin's etude. The books have blank pages, but John claims he's reading *Treasure Island*. The dominoes have no dots, but Jane and Alice play just as if they're real dominoes. The puzzle pieces are all white, but Paul and Richie claim they're putting together a herd of horses."

Madeleine took a deep breath and tried to calm herself. "I pretended to eat dinner. I pretended to hear music. I didn't tell Jane that the dominoes have no dots or John that the book's pages are blank or Paul that the puzzle pieces are plain white. But Miss Simpson says I shouldn't *need* to pretend. What else can I do?"

"It's difficult for you to understand what you're experiencing," Alfred said, "but—"

Madeleine forgot her manners and interrupted. "I don't want to understand. I want to go home."

Alfred sat on a step. "Sit beside me a moment."

Madeleine was tired, so she did as he asked.

"You need to think of the school as a training place."

"Training for what?"

"You're in transition, Madeleine."

"You're speaking in riddles."

Alfred sighed. "I'm not supposed to explain. You're expected to find out for yourself."

"What if I can't?"

"It may take a long time."

"Please at least tell me what I must do before I'm allowed to go home. Whatever it is, I'll do it."

Alfred patted her shoulder. "I can't tell you that, Madeleine. Miss Simpson is the one to ask . . . but she won't tell you either."

Madeleine lowered her head to her knees and began to cry.

"It's easier for some than for others." Alfred paused

a moment and added, "It was very hard for me too." He stood up then and took Madeleine's arm. "Allow me to take you to your room. It's not good for you to overtire yourself."

Madeleine was indeed tired, even more tired than when she was sick. Perhaps she was having a relapse. Mama often warned her about exerting herself after a sickness. "This is a convalescent home, isn't it, Alfred? I'm in training to improve my health. When I'm better, I'll eat real food and read real books like the others. I'll hear music again."

"Just be patient, Madeleine."

She left Alfred at the door and entered the dim room. All the beds were empty except Benjamin's. The other children were still downstairs playing their games.

She looked around for a nightgown. She even looked under her pillow but couldn't find one. She looked at Benjamin to see what he was wearing. Fully clothed except for the shoes he'd lost, he lay on his back, his hands folded on his chest and his eyes closed.

Something about his position bothered Madeleine. She lay down and found herself on her back, hands folded on her chest, just like Benjamin. She always slept on her side and tried to curl up now, but the bed was too narrow and hard. She rolled over onto her stomach but soon found it impossible to sleep in any position.

Benjamin spoke out of the darkness. "Have you figured it out yet?" he whispered.

"Yes." Madeleine tried to sound confident. "We're here to recover from our illness. If we do as we're told, we'll soon be allowed to go home."

"Do you believe that?"

"Of course. Don't you?"

"No."

"Tell me your explanation then."

"Well, if we're recovering, why haven't they fed us a proper meal? We haven't even been given a glass of water. Don't you think that's strange?"

"I'm not hungry yet," Madeleine said. "I'm certain tomorrow will be different. We'll be given a big breakfast and a dose of tonic. We'll play outside in the fresh air. We might even—"

"For heaven's sake, hush." Benjamin sat up and faced her. "Don't you understand? We're here to recover from life."

"That's what I said."

"No, it's not what you said. Or it's not what you meant."

Madeleine lay very still. She clasped her hands tightly

as if she were praying. Perhaps she was praying for Benjamin to go back to sleep. To stop talking. He was scaring her.

"You know what?" she asked him. "I don't like you anymore. You are *not* invited to my birthday party."

Benjamin laughed. "Birthday party? You'll never have another birthday. There won't be a party."

"Horrid boy. I hate you. I detest you!" Madeleine pressed her fingers in her ears to silence Benjamin's voice.

"We are *dead*, Madeleine. *D-E-A-D*. Dead."

"Be quiet! That's not true." Madeleine sobbed. She didn't care who heard her or if she was disturbing anyone.

Suddenly the other children surrounded Madeleine's bed. Alice stroked Madeleine's hair. Jane held her hand. Paul, John, and Richie looked at her with sad faces.

"Benjamin's right," Jane whispered. "Deep down inside, you know it's true."

"No," Madeleine wept. "You're wrong. I'm going home soon. I'm having a party, and Papa has promised to give me a pony. Mama has ordered a beautiful pink silk dress for me."

Jane tightened her grip on Madeleine's hand. "You must give up these fancies, dearest. As Benjamin says, we're here to recover from life. That's why we go through the motions of being alive. It's a way of preparing ourselves to leave this world and move on to the next."

Madeleine struggled to sit up. If only she could wake from this terrible dream, she'd find herself at home in her own bed. But Jane refused to let go of her hand.

Miss Simpson gently pulled Jane away. "Please go to your beds, children. I'll deal with Madeleine."

Madeleine pressed her back to the wall. The other children must have been disturbed by the scene she'd made. They lay quietly on their beds, leaving her alone with Miss Simpson, who surely was very angry with her.

"Now, Madeleine," Miss Simpson said, "I had hoped you'd learn the truth slowly, but Benjamin is a clever boy. He must have figured it out by himself and then told you."

"Yes, miss." Benjamin spoke from the shadows. "It made me sad to see her fooling herself. I'm sorry if I did wrong."

"It's all right, dear," Miss Simpson said. "But I'm afraid it's been a dreadful shock for Madeleine."

She leaned over Madeleine and stroked her forehead gently. Her hand was cool, and Madeleine found it comforting. Slowly, she relaxed.

"Sleep now," Miss Simpson told her. "We'll talk tomorrow. I know you have many questions, but I believe you'll be happy with us. Soon you'll depart, perhaps with Benjamin or Jane, perhaps alone, but when you go, you won't be afraid."

Madeleine lay on her back and closed her eyes. She felt herself drifting into sleep. Tomorrow, she'd ask Miss Simpson about this strange place. She'd ask what lay ahead, she'd ask . . . But she was too tired now to think of the questions.

THE LITTLE BLUE JACKET

t was Steven's idea to play hide-and-seek in the graveyard. Everybody went along with him because he was
the leader.

I don't mean we elected him or anything. That was just
the way it was. He was the tallest and the strongest, and
he always thought of the best stuff to do — stuff that often
got us into trouble. When we were playing hooky, one of
my dad's friends saw us down by the creek and reported
us. We were caught by the school secretary the day we
climbed up on the roof. An old woman saw us putting
pennies on the train tracks and called the police.

But we didn't always get caught. We got away with
setting off firecrackers behind the church on Sunday, starting a fire by accident, and spray-painting
nasty things on the sidewalk in front of the principal's
house.

So the graveyard it was. But not in the daytime. Of
course not. Too easy by half. We had to sneak out after

dark and meet on the corner of Broad Street and Main at eleven thirty—*p.m.*

"Why so late?" David asked.

"If your folks are asleep, it will be easier to sneak out," Steven told him. "And we'll be in the graveyard at midnight, the perfect time to see ghosts, right?"

I was pretty sure everyone was thinking, *Wrong,* but nobody said a word. We all just nodded like, *Sure, of course, midnight in the graveyard, perfect. Bring on the ghosts.*

"Okay then. Friday night, eleven thirty," Steven said.

"That's Halloween," Martha said. She was the only girl in the gang, but she ran faster than Steven, lied better than I did, and pitched for our Little League team. "I'm not missing trick-or-treating."

"You have plenty of time to do that before we go to the graveyard," Steven told her. "You can share your treats with the ghosts."

We all laughed. Sure, of course, what could be more fun than giving candy to a ghost? I, for one, could think of lots of things that would be more fun, but as usual I kept quiet, and so did everyone else.

The streetlights were on, and our parents expected us to be home in time for dinner, so we split up. Martha and

I walked home together. She lived across the street from me, but the other kids lived a few blocks away in the other direction.

Dead leaves followed Martha and me all the way home, scurrying behind us like goblins. The moon was almost full, and the wind had a sharp edge.

"Michael, do you believe in ghosts?" Martha asked.

"Do you?"

"I asked first, so you have to answer. You can't ask me the same question I asked you."

"Well, I've never seen one, but plenty of people claim they have. So who's to say?" I glanced at her. The brim of her baseball cap hid her eyes. "Do you?"

She shrugged. "When she was little, my grandmother saw her father's ghost."

"Was she scared?"

"No, silly, it was her *father*. He came to see her a week after he died and told her not to cry, he was happy enough, and he'd see her again someday. He was standing at the foot of her bed, and she could see through him, but otherwise, he looked just the same. He was wearing the suit he was buried in."

"Wow, that's amazing."

"Yeah, and then he just disappeared. Zap!"

"So you think ghosts aren't scary?"

"Well, my great-grandfather wasn't scary, but that doesn't mean all ghosts are like him. Some could be scary."

"But probably we won't see any ghosts in the graveyard."

"We might."

I stared at her as if she'd lost her mind. "Do you *want* to see one?"

"Don't you?"

"Are you crazy? Why would you or me or anybody want to see a ghost?"

Martha shrugged and adjusted the brim of her cap. "Aren't you curious about what happens after you die? Do you go to heaven, or do you just hang around on earth, or is it like going to sleep and never waking up? Not even dreaming — or maybe you do dream. What do you think dead people dream about? If they dream."

I was glad to see the porch light of my house. I walked faster, anxious to get away from Martha and her weird questions. "I *never* think about that stuff," I told her. "It's not normal."

"Well, I think about it and I'm normal, so maybe you're the one who's not normal."

I was walking so fast I was almost running. Martha

was mad. I'd insulted her, and she might decide to fight me. She was taller and tougher than I was, and I didn't want to go home with a bloody nose. "Forget it," I yelled. "You're normal; I'm normal; we're all normal. Even the ghosts are normal!"

With that, I ran up the sidewalk and into my house. Before I shut the door, I looked back to see what Martha was doing.

She stood in the middle of the street and stuck her tongue out. Then she laughed and dashed into her house.

That night, I lay in bed and listened to the wind shake my windowpanes. Martha's questions lingered in my head. Do dead people dream? If they do, what do they dream about? Being alive, I guessed. Maybe if you lived a happy life, you had good dreams. Maybe it's like you're still alive. Maybe you don't even know you're dead. You just dream your life over and over again.

But what if you were a mean, miserable person who'd had a terrible life? What would you dream about?

I shut my eyes tight and refused to think about that.

The days passed quickly, all too quickly. Before I was ready for the graveyard, it was Halloween and time for tick-or-treating. Martha and I met up a little before six and headed for the corner of Fifth Street and Elmhurst Drive. She wore a long white sheet with eyes cut out, so she could see. It trailed behind her, making whispery noises in the leaves as if something were following us. Considering where we were going at midnight, it was a bad costume choice.

Steven was dressed like Dracula: black cape, fake fangs, fake blood smeared on his mouth. David was a spaceman, and George was Batman in a flimsy Walmart costume. I was a pirate with an eye patch and a fake parrot. I said "Arrr" so often Steven told me to shut up, so I squawked like a parrot and said, "Pieces of eight, pieces of eight." Steven told me again to shut up, and Martha said I was a very unoriginal pirate, but I kept on blabbering stupid things. Probably because I was so scared of going to the graveyard.

The streets were filled with shadowy shapes of trick-or-treaters, all lugging big plastic garbage bags like ours, laughing and shouting, running from house to house, ringing doorbells, holding out their bags for candy bars and chewing gum and little boxes of raisins, sometimes even pencils or pennies. Steven lunged at every girl and snarled, "I vant to drink your blood." I shouted "Arrr," Martha screamed and moaned and waved her arms around,

David claimed he was from Mars, and George hollered "Shazam!" every time someone gave him candy. Martha told him that's not what Batman says—but George kept saying it anyway.

By the time we quit at eight, we had enough candy for a year, which, if we survived the graveyard, we'd eat in a week. When we parted our separate ways to go home, Steven reminded us to be at the graveyard on time. As if any of us had forgotten.

Martha and I walked down our street without saying much. Even though trick-or-treating was officially over, a few kids raced one another to houses that still had their porch lights on.

"So," Martha said, "are you scared?"

"Of course not." I hoped I didn't sound like I was lying. "Why should I be?"

Martha shrugged. We were in front of her house so she said, "See you in a few hours. Don't be late!"

I watched her run across the street and dart through her front door. I watched a rerun of an old Chuckie movie and went to bed early. Not to sleep. No, I was way too wired to close my eyes. Fully dressed except for my shoes, I got under my covers and read the last Harry Potter book for the third time, but instead of getting involved with

Harry and his friends, I kept looking at the clock on my computer. At first, the time moved so slowly I thought it was broken, but around eleven, the minutes started zooming past. At eleven twenty, I slid quietly out of bed and put on my shoes. Grabbing my flashlight, I tiptoed down the steps. The front door made a lot of noise, so I left by the back door and ran around front to meet Martha.

From the street, I looked at my house, sitting peacefully in the moonlight. Not one light on. I took a quick look at the rest of the neighborhood. The Masons' house was the only one with a light showing. Quickly, I stepped into a shadow and hoped nobody had looked outside and seen me waiting for Martha.

Just as I began to hope she'd chickened out, she darted across the street and joined me. "Sorry," she whispered. "I didn't hear my alarm."

I looked at my glowing watch face. "Hurry, it's almost eleven thirty."

We ran down the sidewalk, chased by flurries of dead, dry leaves. A dog barked from someone's yard, a car cruised past, but no one else was out and about except Martha and me.

When we got to the cemetery, the others were waiting. "Let's go," Steven said. "It's almost midnight."

We slipped through a gap in the cemetery fence. Bleached pale in the moonlight, angels and crosses cast long dark shadows across the grass. The dead lay all around us in every direction. Even though I tried not to, I couldn't stop thinking about zombies. I imagined them creeping toward us from their graves, outnumbering us a hundred to one. If they really existed, we'd be doomed.

Steven led us up a hill, to a huge oak at its top. The tree's lower branches were thicker than my body, and its top hid the stars. Ivy grew up its trunk and clung to its branches, making it look like a giant wearing ragged clothes.

"Okay," Steven said. "Michael, you're it. Count to twelve and then come looking for us."

"Wait a minute!" I squawked. "How come I'm it?"

"Because you were late."

"It was Martha's fault. I was waiting for her."

"Now you've ratted on a friend. Twice the reason to be it."

With that, all of them ran. Even though I was scared, I made myself close my eyes, press my face against the tree, and count to twelve. The faster I found them, the less time I'd be by myself. When I finished counting, the graveyard was absolutely silent—not a giggle, not a whisper, not even a rustle in the bushes. Except for the dead, I might have been the only person there.

Way high up in the sky, a crescent moon cast enough light for me to read the names carved into the stones, but I didn't want to know whose grave I might be stepping on as I ventured away from the giant tree.

"Ready or not," I shouted, "here I come."

Cautiously, I looked behind a tall gravestone. No one hid in its long shadow. I went to the next one. No one there. No one behind Susan, beloved wife, or James, beloved husband. Ahead of me was a mausoleum with an iron gate, the Portman Family's home. I shone my light inside. Nothing there but stone coffins.

On I went. "Martha?" I called. "George? Steven?"

No one answered. The wind blew harder. The limbs of the giant tree behind me rattled like bones. Leaves rushed past, nipping my ankles. Something moved near one of the graves. Ready to pounce, I ran toward it, but no one was there.

I looked around, confused. "David?" He was the smallest of us, and the figure I'd glimpsed was about his size. "Come on out. *I see you.*" I didn't actually see him, but I was too scared to play by the rules.

He giggled. There was a large bush in front of me, and

I knelt down to look under it. I saw him crouching there in the dark. I reached for him. "Come out. It's the rule."

My fingers closed around his arm, and I pulled him toward me. He clung to a branch and fought to stay where he was. "Leave me be, leave me be," he begged in an odd, quavery voice.

"What's wrong with you, David?" I yelled. "I've caught you fair and square. Come out right now!"

"What's up, Michael? You're making enough noise to raise the dead." Steven squatted beside me, laughing at his own joke. Martha knelt beside him and peered under the bush.

"It's David. He won't come out," I told them. "Something must have spooked him."

Steven stared at me. "Are you nuts? David and George got scared and went home. It's only you and me and Martha now."

"Then who's under the bush?"

I laughed to show Steven I knew he was just trying to scare me. At any moment, David and George would jump out from behind the bush, shouting *Boo!*

When Steven and Martha looked at each other and laughed, I got mad. I tightened my grip on David's arm and pulled with all my strength.

I felt him let go of the branch and started dragging him out into the moonlight. His arm was thin and brittle, fragile enough to snap if I pulled too hard. I relaxed my grip and felt him slip away from me. Instead of my friend, all I held was a ragged blue jacket, old and musty and way too small even for David. Three brass buttons dangled loosely from the front, but the top button was missing.

All three of us scrambled away from the little jacket and stared at it as if it might be dangerous.

"I told you David went home," Steven said. "He was wearing his scruffy old red parka, not a creepy thing like that." He nudged the blue jacket with the toe of his running shoe.

"Well, *someone* was under there. That jacket proves it." I looked at Martha and Steven. "If it wasn't David, who was it?"

Martha shook her head. "I don't know."

"Me either." Steven frowned. "What kind of kid would wear a filthy rag like this?"

"Whoever he was, why was he hiding under this bush?" Martha asked.

"And where did he go?" Steven knelt down to peer under the bush again. "Give me your flashlight, Michael."

I watched him shine it slowly across the ground. "There's a hole in there," he said. "It could be a tunnel."

"Big enough for a little kid to crawl down?" I asked.

"Probably." Steven stood up. "One of us should crawl in there and check it out. I'd do it myself, but I'm too big."

Martha took the flashlight and wiggled under the bush. Although she was too tall to crawl into the tunnel, she shined the light down the hole. "Look at this." She held up a brass button. "It matches the other buttons on the jacket. He must have gone this way."

"Let's see where the tunnel comes out," Steven said.

We walked around the bush and looked for another entrance to the tunnel, but there was no sign of one. Or the boy who owned the jacket.

While Steven and I continued to look for the tunnel, Martha examined the tombstones. "Come here," she called. "And look at this."

She shone the light on a tombstone almost hidden under the bush that had grown up around it. Tracing the letters with her finger, she read, "In loving memory of our beloved son, Thomas Livingston, gone but not forgotten. 14 April 1868–18 June 1874."

"So?" Steven looked at her. "I mean it's sad and all that, but what's it got to do with the tunnel?"

Clutching the button, she whispered, "Suppose the jacket belongs to Thomas Livingston. He was only six years old when he died, just the right size for the jacket."

"That's crazy," Steven said. "Dead kids don't hide under bushes."

"Look at the bush, Steven," Martha went on. "It practically covers the tombstone. I bet you anything that tunnel ends in Thomas Livingston's grave."

I shivered. "Don't say that, Martha. If it's true, I just held a ghost by its arm."

"For crying out loud," Steven said. "There's no such thing as ghosts."

"But, Steven, his arm was as hard as a bone. And his voice—it sounded like a low growl."

Steven looked at me. Then he looked at Martha. Finally, he looked at the jacket lying on the grass. "You know something? There has to be another explanation."

"But what?" Martha asked. "If he'd been real, we'd have found him by now. And besides, what would a boy be doing all by himself in a graveyard on Halloween night?"

"A kid as dumb as we are?" I asked. The three brass buttons shone in the moonlight. The jacket was so small, so ragged, so dirty. I turned my head, unable to look at it.

I was ashamed to admit even to myself that I was scared to touch it.

Steven didn't look at the jacket either. "Now that David and George are gone," he said, "hide-and-seek isn't much fun. You need more than three for a good game, don't you think?"

Without waiting for us to answer, he added, "I don't know about you guys, but I'm cold. I think I'll go home." Hands in pockets, Steven sauntered away. From the back, he had the look of a person who wanted to run but didn't for fear someone might think he was scared.

I was about to follow him, but Martha stopped me.

"Wait, Michael. We should give his jacket back."

I watched her wriggle under the bush again, jacket gripped in one fist. With her mouth close to the hole in the ground, she whispered, "Thomas, if you're listening, we're sorry we scared you. We thought you were one of our friends playing a trick on us."

She pressed her ear to the hole. She nodded her head a few times. "Of course we'll give you your jacket—and the button that fell off."

She listened again and then said, "Yes, I understand. You must be very lonesome."

When she stopped talking to listen again, I was so curious I pushed my way to her side.

Martha frowned at me and put her finger to her lips. To Thomas she said, "Yes, I know you don't want us to see you. I understand that, but what if I visit you sometimes? You can stay in your tunnel and I'll read stories to you or tell you about the world, whatever you'd like to know. It has to be in the daytime though. It's hard for me to get out of the house after dark."

I got as close to the hole as she'd let me and tried to hear Thomas. He spoke in such a low whispery voice I couldn't understand a word he said.

Martha pushed the jacket and the button to the edge of the hole. Almost immediately, the jacket disappeared. Then a small hand reached out and grabbed the button.

"We'll leave you now," Martha told Thomas. "I'll come back soon with a book—maybe *Treasure Island*. It's about pirates and buried treasure. You'll like it."

I backed out from under the bush and Martha slowly followed.

"It's so sad," she whispered. "Poor Thomas. I feel so sorry for him."

I looked at the bush's black shape huddled over Thomas Livingston's grave. "Let's go home, Martha."

At the cemetery gate, she turned to me. "What do you think about ghosts now?"

"I hope Thomas Livingston is having sweet dreams," I told her.

THE LAST HOUSE ON CRESCENT ROAD

The first time I saw him, I was throwing a ball against the school wall. It was a warm summer evening. The sun had already set, and the first stars were coming out, one by one, so slowly you could still count them, but there was enough light to practice pitching and catching.

I was in a pretty bad mood. We'd lost our first game, and it was my fault. First of all, I'd struck out when the bases were loaded. Then, as if that wasn't bad enough, I'd missed an easy fly. When I finally caught up with the ball, I threw it short, and as a result, the other team got four runs. By the time we slunk off the field, the score was twelve to five.

"Way to go, Barnes," Travis O'Neil muttered. From the way he was scowling at me, it was easy to see who he blamed. Not himself, the champion batter, but me — Adam Barnes, number one klutz, strikeout champ, and all-around jerk.

And it wasn't just Travis who was mad. I got it from everybody. The coach yelled at me, my father yelled at me,

Mrs. O'Neil yelled at me. My friends were so angry they wouldn't even talk to me. Public enemy number one—that's who I was. In the old days, I would have been tarred and feathered and run out of Calvertville on a rail.

So here I was, all by myself, hurling ball after ball at a brick wall, missing more than I caught, trying not to cry, telling myself people would forget about today. One game—so what? The summer wasn't over, not yet. Surely I'd improve.

Angry at myself, I threw the ball as hard as I could. It came bouncing back, high and fast. I jumped for it, felt it brush my glove and sail on past. When I turned to run after it, there he was, a red-haired boy grinning at me.

"Looking for this?" He hurled the ball straight at me, but instead of trying to catch it, I ducked. Like Travis, this kid knew how to throw a ball hard enough to sting your hand right through a glove.

I expected him to laugh—Travis would have—but he just stood there staring at me. He was around my age, eleven or thereabouts, built skinny and short. A total stranger.

"Aren't you going to get the ball?" he asked.

I wheeled around, found it in the tall grass, and turned back to the boy. He was pounding one fist in the palm of a baseball glove, an old one, real leather it looked like. Behind him, a bike leaned against its kickstand. It had fat balloon tires, the kind that make no noise. No wonder I hadn't heard him coming.

"Throw it here," the boy said.

I tossed the ball, and he caught it as easily as a frog catches a fly. Barely moved. Just swung his hand out, and the ball dropped into his glove. Plock.

This time, he threw it nice and gentle. When I caught it, he seemed pleased. Back and forth, back and forth, the ball swung through the dusk. Sometimes I missed, sometimes I threw badly and it fell short or went too wide, but most of the time, he managed to catch it. He had the same grace Travis had, a way of making every move look easy.

When it was too dark to see the ball, we sat on the school steps. In the maple near us, locusts buzzed like children repeating lessons, droning on and on monotonously, stopping and starting, stopping and starting.

I glanced at the red-haired boy, but he was staring at the maple as if he were trying to calculate its height.

He must have felt me watching him, because he turned to me and asked an odd question. "How long has that tree been there?"

I did a little mental arithmetic. "About thirty years."

"As long as that?" He looked as if he didn't believe me.

Had I figured wrong? Next to baseball, arithmetic was my worst subject, but thirty years was thirty years.

"My dad's sixth grade class planted it," I told him. "It commemorates something, I forget what."

A breeze rustled the maple's leaves, making a sound like girls whispering in the back row. The boy cocked his head and listened for a moment. "What's your name?" he asked.

"Adam Barnes," I said, and he nodded as if I'd given the right answer.

"I'm Charles," he said.

"Are you new in town?"

He shook his head. "No, I've been here for a while."

That surprised me. Calvertville was a small place, and I'd never seen Charles before.

He must have guessed what I was thinking because he added, "I keep to myself."

Before I could think of another question, Charles asked one. "Do you play here every night?"

"I wouldn't call it play," I said. "This year my baseball team has a new coach. Mr. Stohl's really tough. He yells at me all the time, says I don't try. I'm always dropping the ball, I can't throw straight, I can't hit. Today was our first game and we lost. Everybody said it was my fault."

I glanced at Charles. He was staring at the maple again, but I knew he was listening to me.

"I want to get so good I'll surprise everybody," I told him. "You know, win the game with a great catch or a spectacular home run. Like a kid in a book or a movie."

Scared he'd laugh, I let my voice trail off. It was a dumb idea. Charles had just seen me fumble almost every ball he threw. I was a klutz. He knew it; I knew it; everybody knew it.

To my surprise, Charles smiled as if he understood. "You won't learn much bouncing a ball off a wall, Adam."

"I know, but my dad doesn't have time to help me. And my friends think I'm hopeless. This stupid wall is all I have."

"What if I meet you here every night?" Charles asked. "I'm pretty good. I bet I could teach you a lot."

"Do you mean it?"

He grinned and hopped on his old Schwinn. "See you tomorrow," he called as he pedaled down Calvert Road. "Same time, same place."

• • •

The next evening, I got to the school before Charles. While I waited for him, I threw the ball against the wall, missing my own throws more often than not. Just as I was about to give up and go home, I saw him pedaling silently toward me, hunched over the handlebars of his Schwinn. Braking to a stop in a cloud of dust and gravel, he jumped off the bike and let it fall on its side. The noise bounced back to us from the wall. It was the loudest sound I'd ever heard Charles make.

"You're late," I said.

"Sometimes it's hard to get away." He slipped his hand into his glove, and I threw the ball to him.

Back it came, fast and true, but instead of catching it, I ducked like I had last night. "Don't throw so hard."

"You're scared it's going to hit you in the face," Charles said, "and break your glasses. Right?"

I nodded. He was absolutely correct.

Tossing his mitt at me, Charles said, "Try this. It's my lucky glove."

It landed in the dirt at my feet. Except for its age, the glove looked pretty ordinary. The leather had a mellow smell, a mix of sweat and old shoes and dirt. When I slid my hand inside, it felt soft and warm and slightly damp.

I handed Charles my glove and watched him put it on.

He flexed his fingers and pounded his fist into the palm. "No wonder you can't catch," he said scornfully. "This is a lousy glove."

I shrugged. "Dad says there's no sense wasting money on somebody like me."

"Wear mine," Charles said, "and you'll be good. I swear you will."

I bent my fingers like he had and struck my fist against the padding. "They don't make them like this anymore," I said. "How long have you had it?"

"I don't remember." Backing away, Charles spit on the ball and rubbed it between his palms. "Come on," he said, "let's try again. Remember—with my glove on, you can't miss."

I flinched, I shut my eyes, but the ball landed in my cupped glove—*whack*. Closing my other hand over it, I stared at Charles. "I caught it!" I yelled. "I caught it!"

"Now throw it to me," he shouted. "Come on, don't just stand there gawking! Pretend there's a guy running for home and you have to stop him."

By the time it was dark and we had to stop, I'd caught every ball Charles had thrown. Even the hard ones. Maybe he was right about the glove being lucky. It sure seemed that way. If I could do this well in a game, Travis might actually be impressed, Dad would be pleased, and Mr. Stohl would quit calling me Butterfingers.

As if he read my thoughts, Charles said, "You can keep the glove for a while if you like. I don't need it."

Hugging it to my chest, I leaned toward him. "Why don't you join our team, Charles? You're even better than Travis. Mr. Stohl would give a million bucks to get somebody as good as you."

Without looking at me, Charles said, "I wish I could, but I'm not allowed to play anymore. They won't let me."

I waited for him to explain, but instead he got to his feet. "It's late," he said. "I have to go home."

Standing under the maple, I watched him ride away. Calvert Road was lined with trees. In the summer, their leaves made a shade so dense it was like looking into a tunnel. In seconds, the Schwinn was out of sight.

Charles and I played ball together for a couple of weeks. Sometimes we practiced catching and throwing; sometimes we practiced hitting. He taught me lots of tricks—how to track the ball with my eyes, when to swing, when to let it go by, how to follow through.

But his biggest trick had nothing to do with baseball. What he was absolutely best at was keeping himself a secret. Who was he? Where did he live? I didn't even know his last name.

"How come I never see you anywhere but here?" I asked him one night.

We were sitting on the school steps, shoulder to shoulder.

Charles glanced at me, but he didn't answer. The streetlight on the corner turned his skin as pale as skim milk.

"I'm always looking for you," I went on. "At the swimming pool, the park, the shopping center. What do you do all day? Where do you go?"

"Not much. I'm kind of a night person, so I sleep late. I hate swimming pools, and shopping centers bore me. What I like best is riding my bike around town in the dark —no people. Peaceful, quiet. Sometimes I play ball with kids like you."

I still didn't get Charles. His answers to my questions were vague, strange, maybe a little just this side of weird. But he was a darn good ballplayer. Minutes passed, and Charles said nothing more. He sat beside me and gazed at the maple.

"I remember when I was taller than that tree," he said suddenly.

"Oh, sure." When he didn't respond to my sarcasm, I

added, "Tell me another one, Charles. That tree's a whole lot older than you are."

He looked at me then, and something in his eyes told me to shut up. Uneasily, I edged away from him. Maybe he had problems I didn't know about. Didn't even want to know about. A boy who wasn't allowed to join a ball team, a boy who never went anywhere in the daytime.

"Sorry," I mumbled, but I wasn't sure why I was apologizing.

Ignoring me, Charles picked up his bike. Hanging my baseball glove on the handlebar, he said, "I'm not sure I can meet you here again, Adam."

I grabbed his arm to stop him. "But we have a big game tomorrow," I said. "I was hoping you'd come."

"I wish I could," he said. "You can't imagine how much I'd like to be there."

He started to pedal away, and I ran after him. "What about your glove?"

Charles glanced over his shoulder. "Use it tomorrow," he yelled. "Then take it to my house and give it to my father. Tell him about the game. He'll be expecting you."

He was pedaling faster, vanishing into the black shade of the trees. "But I don't know where you live," I shouted.

"The last house on Crescent Road," he called back. "Ask for Mr. Bradford."

I chased him down Calvert Road. Just ahead, his white shirt glimmered. The red reflector on his rear fender gleamed in a car's headlights. Then he was gone. Just like that. I'd never seen anyone disappear so fast.

Charles would have been proud of me. Not only did I hit a home run when the bases were loaded, but I caught a fly at the bottom of the last inning that sewed up the game. Mr. Stohl gave me a bear hug, Travis invited me to his house for pizza, and Dad offered to buy me the best glove he could afford.

"I didn't realize you'd been using such a shabby old thing," he said.

It was a hot afternoon, but as soon as I'd showered and changed my clothes, I walked all the way to Crescent Road by myself. It was on the other side of town, and I was soaked with sweat when I rang the bell. While I waited for someone to open the door, I leaned against the porch railing. The air was sweet with the smell of roses and freshly cut grass. Bees hummed, a bird sang, and a cat stalked across the lawn, its eye on a squirrel.

Of Charles, there was no sign.

Finally, I heard footsteps, sort of slow and shuffle-y. "All right, all right," someone muttered, "I'm coming."

The door opened, and an old man peered out at me. Scanty white hair, eyes as deep set as a turtle's, bent back, gnarled hands—he looked as if he was expecting me.

"Is Charles here?" I asked.

The old man shook his head. "I'm Mr. Bradford," he said. "Charles's father."

Before I could tell him why I'd come, Mr. Bradford said, "You've brought his glove, haven't you?"

I held it toward him. "Charles told me to give it to you," I said. "I was hoping he'd be home to hear about the game."

Mr. Bradley took the glove and cradled it as if it were a newborn baby. "The bases were loaded and you hit a home run," he said. "Then, at the bottom of the last inning, you caught the fly that won the game."

I stared at him. "How did you know?"

Mr. Bradford opened the door wider and stepped aside to let me in. For the first time, I noticed the old woman behind him. When I realized she was crying, I edged away, but she reached out and took my hand.

"Please come with me," she said softly.

Too embarrassed to protest, I followed her upstairs to a small room at the end of the hall. The late-afternoon sunlight slanted through the windows and sparkled on a row of trophies. The walls were covered with pictures of old-timers like Hank Aaron and Sandy Koufax. A faded Baltimore Orioles pennant hung over a neatly made bed. Several cigar boxes full of baseball cards sat on the bureau next to a stack of comic books.

Outside, a lawn mower sputtered, a dog barked, an airplane droned. Ordinary summer noises — but for some reason, they didn't sound right. In Charles's silent room, I felt like an archeologist looking at things untouched for centuries.

Squeezing my hand, Mrs. Bradford said, "You're not the first boy to bring my son's glove home."

Despite the heat, a shiver ran up and down my spine. "What do you mean?"

Mr. and Mrs. Bradford gazed at each other. "The telling's so hard," the old woman said.

"It doesn't get easier no matter how often we explain," her husband said. "But you tell it best, Hazel."

I looked from one to the other. Mrs. Bradford wiped her eyes and took a deep breath. "Thirty years ago today, Charles hit a home run when the bases were loaded. At the bottom of the last inning, he caught the fly that won the game."

She paused and glanced at her husband, but he had his back to us. "Charles came rushing home on his bike, fast and reckless, too excited to be careful."

Her voice faltered, and Mr. Bradford turned and put his arm around her shoulders. "Before he got here, a car hit him in front of the elementary school," he said. "Every now and then, he sends a boy home with his glove. They all tell me the same story about the game."

"Are you saying Charles is dead?" I whispered.

"You don't believe us," Mrs. Bradford said. "No one ever does."

I backed away from them one step at a time, finding the stairs with my feet like a blind man. My knees were so weak I thought I'd fall. It was a trick, I told myself, a hoax Charles had dreamed up and talked his parents into participating in.

Mr. Bradford followed me to the door. "Go to the school," he said. "There's a maple by the front steps. Read the bronze plaque."

I ran across the neatly trimmed lawn and dashed up Crescent Road without saying goodbye or looking back. At first, my only thought was to go home, but as I passed the school, I saw my old baseball glove hanging from a branch on the maple. That Charles—what a weird sense of humor he had. Boy, would he laugh when he found out I'd almost fallen for his joke.

Convinced he was hiding behind the tree, I called to him. My voice bounced back from the school's wall. The only other sound was the cooing of a mourning dove.

"Where are you, Charles?" I circled the maple, but there was no sign of him. "Quit fooling around, darn it. Come on out."

Fed up with Charles's tricks, I grabbed my glove from the limb, but it was so cold, it slipped from my fingers and landed in the tall grass. When I reached for it, I saw the bronze plaque.

Remembering what Mr. Bradford had said, I felt my throat tighten. I'd noticed the plaque before, but I'd never bothered to read the inscription. It was from long ago, I'd thought, way back when my parents were kids. Nothing to do with me. Now I knelt down and smoothed the grass away.

"In Memory of our Beloved Classmate Charles Robert Bradford," I read. "March 8, 1962–July 17, 1973."

As I stared at the words, a shadow fell across the plaque. "Here you are, Adam. I've been looking for you."

Startled by my father's voice, I scrambled to my feet. Pointing at the plaque, I said, "He died thirty years ago today."

"Charlie Bradford," Dad said softly. "He was the best ballplayer in Calvertville. If he'd lived, he'd be a pro today." Turning to me, he added, "You reminded me of him this afternoon, Adam. The way you hit that homer —straight across the creek just like he used to. And the fly you caught. You were Charlie all over again. The champ."

To hide my tears, I slung my arms around Dad and hugged him hard. We stayed like that for a while. It was just about the closest we'd ever been.

Before we left the playground, I looked back. For a moment, I thought I saw Charles leaning against the maple's trunk, but it must have been a trick of the light. When I stared hard, he vanished.

"We'll get a new glove tomorrow," Dad said. "Real leather. This vinyl feels as cold as a dead man's hand."

He tossed the glove into a trashcan and slung one arm around my shoulders. We walked home that way, slow and easy, watching the stars come out one by one.

THE THIRTEENTH PIGEON

t was raining when I woke up. Dull, gray, almost frozen rain hitting the windows like pebbles. Too dreary to get out of bed. Too dreary to get dressed. Too dreary to go to school. I pulled the covers over my head and tried to go back to sleep.

I had a good reason for wanting to stay home, and the weather had nothing to do with it. Today was the day Walter Krumgold had promised to pound me flat for laughing at a dumb mistake he'd made in math. Could I help it if he was a moron and I was a genius? But sadly, even a genius can make a mistake and laugh when he shouldn't.

Mom yelled from downstairs, "Richard, what are you doing up there?"

I felt like saying I was preparing to die, but Mom wouldn't have believed me. I couldn't even tell her about Walter's plans for me. For one thing, she thought Walter was a sweet boy who would never hurt anyone. For another, she'd say I'd brought it on myself—as usual.

Unfortunately, that was true. I had a knack for saying

the wrong thing at the wrong time to the wrong person. But should I be killed for it?

So I pulled on my clothes, ate my soggy cereal and toast, grabbed my bookbag and jacket, and trudged down the sidewalk in the cold rain.

At the bottom of the hill, I saw the kids waiting for the bus. Walter was in the middle of them, laughing and pounding his right fist into the palm of his left hand. Showing what he meant to do to me, I guessed. Nobody would come to my defense. For one thing, I didn't have many friends, and, even if I did, who would risk making Walter mad? In fact, I had a feeling they were all looking forward to watching Walter at work. Nothing like a good fight to start the day right.

At that moment, the school bus pulled up to the stop. Just as I was about to run down the hill to catch it, I realized that nobody had noticed me. Not Walter, not my so-called classmates, not the bus driver. If I didn't get on that bus, Walter couldn't beat me up. Better yet, if I didn't go to school, I wouldn't have to make up a lame excuse for not handing in the ten-page social studies report that I hadn't even started writing.

So I stepped behind a tree and watched the bus leave. I thought I saw Walter's disappointed face peering out the back window as if he hoped to see me running down the street, shouting, *Wait for me!*

When the bus turned the corner and disappeared from sight, I looked back at my nice warm, dry house. If only Mom had a job, the house would be empty and I could hole up and play video games all day. But no. Mom was a stay-at-home mother with no plans to go anywhere.

I looked at my watch. The library would open in two hours. I'd just have to hang out somewhere until then. The drugstore, I guessed. It was just across the street from the library.

Walking along the road was too risky—a teacher or a neighbor might drive by and see me. So I decided to take the long way through the park. Nobody would be there on a day like this.

Sloshing through puddles, I took a side path leading through dripping trees. Soon I was soaked and shivering and even more miserable. Just as I'd thought, the park was deserted. No mothers pushing baby strollers, no kids zooming by on inline skates, no skateboarders whooping it up by the fountain, no bicyclists shouting "On your left" before zipping past on their racers. Just me and the rain and the squirrels darting from tree to tree.

Then I saw her—a strange old woman sitting on a

bench, tossing birdseed to a dozen or so pigeons at her feet. A bag lady, I guessed, dressed in ragged clothes faded to a mossy gray. Homeless probably. Maybe even crazy.

She was just as wet as I was. You'd think she might worry about catching pneumonia or something. But no, she just sat there, scattering seed for those stupid pigeons. Useless birds — dirty, clumsy, greedy. "Rats with feathers," my father called them. "Disease spreaders," my mother said, "crawling with lice."

Suddenly I got the bright idea to throw stones at the pigeons. Not to hurt them, of course. Just to scare them. The old woman hadn't seen me. She wouldn't know what was going on. Quietly I bent down and picked up a handful of pebbles.

The first pebble I threw hit an especially ugly pigeon. It let out a squawk and waddled under a bush.

The old woman looked up, her eyes fierce. "Who threw that?" she cried.

I stayed behind my tree and tried not to laugh. As soon as the old woman returned her attention to the pigeons, I threw another pebble. *Squawk! Squawk!* The dumb birds scattered, some flying up into trees, some diving under bushes. It was really hard not to laugh now.

Again, the old woman looked around and scowled.

"Throw one more stone, and whoever you are, I guarantee you'll be sorry."

If I'd had any sense, I would have sneaked off to the drugstore right there and then and gotten myself a hot chocolate, but I couldn't resist throwing another pebble. At *her* this time, since the pigeons were out of reach. The pebble was no bigger than the tip of my little finger. It landed in her lap.

I doubt she even felt the pebble, but she leaped to her feet as if she'd been shot. "I warned you, boy!" she cried. "I told you not to throw another one. Now come out from behind that tree!"

I turned to run, but instead of going where I meant to go, I found myself walking toward the old woman. Very slowly, dragging my feet. I stopped in front of her, much closer than I wanted to be.

She seized my arm with a cold, scrawny hand, chilling me to the bone. Studying my face with red-rimmed eyes set deep in her skull, she said, "How dare you throw stones at me and my helpless dear ones?"

"I'm sorry," I muttered, eager to be gone, to have my hot chocolate, to head for the library and cruise the internet. "I was just teasing you."

"Teasing," she echoed. "Just teasing. They all say that."

She widened her mouth into a grin that revealed big yellow teeth crowded together in a crooked line. "Suppose I was to tease you, boy?"

"I said I was sorry." I tried to pull away from her, but she tightened her grip on my arm. "Let me go. You're hurting me."

"But I'm just teasing you," she said, baring her hideous teeth again.

"Please," I whispered. "My mother is coming to meet me. She should be here any minute."

"Oh, I doubt that," the old woman said. "She thinks you're in school, don't she?"

"No. I had a dental appointment, and she—"

She shook me angrily. "I hate liars."

"I'm not—"

She shook me again, harder this time. Around my feet, the pigeons cooed and pecked at the seed and ruffled their feathers. The one I'd hit with the stone jabbed my shoe with his sharp beak.

The old woman smiled down at the pigeons. "This boy don't know who I am, does he?"

Several pigeons puffed up their chests and strutted toward me. Heads bobbing viciously, they joined the first pigeon and pecked my feet. Others cooed and milled around me. I was scared now. The pigeons seemed smarter and meaner than I'd ever suspected.

The old woman went on talking to the pigeons. "I doubt he's ever met a witch," she said. "In fact, I bet he don't even believe in witches."

The pigeons made a sound like laughter and crowded around my ankles, trapping me.

My heart thumped against my ribs. "You're crazy," I shouted. "Let me go!"

The old woman grinned at the pigeons. "Should we let him go? Or should we keep him?"

"Help!" I shouted. "Help, help!"

"Go ahead, boy, shout all you want," the old woman said. "Nobody comes to the park on days like this, except witches and bad boys."

"You're not a witch," I shouted at her. "You're just a crazy old lady. Let me go or else!"

"Or else?" The old woman laughed. "Or else what?"

"I'll tell my mother about you. I'll tell my father. I'll tell the police."

The old woman nudged the pigeons gently with her pointy-toed shoes. "Me and my little friends have heard that before, ain't we, boys?"

The pigeons drew closer together and cooed. They

weren't laughing now. No, they sounded lost and sad and forlorn.

The old woman raised her head and smiled at me. All her yellow teeth gleamed. "I had thirteen pigeons yesterday," she told me softly, "but I ate one for supper last night. Now I need to replace him."

A ripping, piercing pain shot through my body like lightning, fierce and keen. I felt myself shrinking, condensing, changing shape. Where my arms had been, I saw wings. Where my shoes had been, I saw ugly pink feet. My nose grew sharp and hard. Feathers burst through my skin.

"I reckon you believe me now," the old witch said. Gathering her bags, she got to her feet. "Come along now, dears."

The other pigeons pressed in around me, their beady eyes probing mine. I had no choice but to go along with them, my head bobbing, my pink toes splayed on the wet sidewalk, cooing mournfully.

• • •

AFTERWORD: WHAT MAKES ME WRITE GHOST STORIES?

Ah, if only I knew the answer to that question. We don't always know where we get our ideas or why we write a particular story. Sometimes I think stories find us. The story begins with a whisper in our inner ear. It might be a what-if question; it might be a memory; it might be a place we've seen or visited. The possibilities are endless. Once we hear that whisper, something clicks, and our imagination goes to work.

But why, oh why, do I hear so many whispers from ghosts? I must be drawn to them—or them to me.

Maybe I write ghost stories because I was so scared of everything when I was little: the dark, the long-armed witch under my bed, the basement and its spooky shadows, the monster creeping up the steps to my bedroom, the wolf hiding in my closet, graveyards, dead people. Yes, I was probably the biggest scaredy-cat crybaby in my hometown.

It should be no surprise that I never read scary stories as a child. I preferred dog stories, funny family stories, and adventure stories. If I'd come across *Wait Till Helen Comes* when I was ten, I wouldn't have touched it. Nancy Drew was the limit then.

But here I am, grown older and still scared of many things, writing stories that would have terrified the child I once was.

Something about the supernatural fascinates me. Maybe its appeal stems from my childhood fears and my attempts to overcome them as I grew older. In sixth grade, for instance, I noticed that my friend Rusty was reading Sherlock Holmes stories. He and I had spent the previous summer reading the Hardy Boys series, one after another, bingeing on them—Rusty owned the whole set. I considered them a step up from Nancy Drew because they were scarier.

So I thought, in the sixth grade, if Rusty was reading Sherlock Holmes stories, they must be the next step up from the Hardy Boys. Rusty and I were among the best readers in our class. If he read Sherlock Holmes stories, I'd be brave and read them too.

Off to the library I went and checked out a volume of Sherlock Holmes. Some of the stories terrified me, especially *The Hound of the Baskervilles,* which played uncannily on all my fears—desolate places, dense fog, a huge howling, murderous dog, mysterious messages and threats, sinister goings-on, and a brand-new one: quicksand. How had I missed worrying about slowly suffocating in quicksand? A horrible death—one to add to my long list of terrible ways to die.

In seventh grade, still looking for the next step up, I tackled the master of scary stories, Edgar Allan Poe, and shivered and shook over "The Telltale Heart," "The Black Cat," and "The Murders in the Rue Morgue," among others. In eighth grade, Miss Bell assigned an illustrated book report. I chose Poe's "The Masque of the Red Death," a truly frightening account of an uninvited guest, Death himself, who attends a masked ball and infects everyone there with the fatal Red Death. My illustrations, particularly of death, are surprisingly scary.

By the time I began high school, I'd become an avid reader of scary stories. In twelfth grade, my favorite teacher, Miss Hardy, gave our English class an assignment to write a short story. When I handed mine to her, I was sure she'd love it. But when Miss Hardy returned our stories, she gave mine a B-. I was shocked. In my opinion, "Storm" was an amazing story. My friends agreed. One of them unofficially crossed out the B- and changed it to A+.

Here is what I wrote for Miss Hardy:

STORM
Mary Downing
English, Period II
Miss Hardy
6 March 1956

Grade B-

The road stretched ahead, black and empty, devoid of any life. The loneliness of the countryside seemed to draw itself like a cloak around the car, and its complete solitude depressed me.

Then, to add to the darkness, the storm started. It began as a fine drizzle but increased to a raging gale, pounding on the car with unabated fury. Soon the winding road was enshrouded in rain and darkness, and fearing the twists and turns, I stopped to await the storm's cease.

As I sat there, a feeling crept over me; I was certain that there was someone, or something, in the darkness outside. I was aware of a fear of the unknown as I listened to the raging voice of the wind about me. Then I saw a flickering light gleaming among the trees tossing in the gale. A feeling of relief swept over me. A light meant people, a house, and perhaps hospitality. But still an undefinable fear tugged at my heart.

Brushing the uncanny feeling aside, I pushed the car door open and ran through the night. There seemed to be an almost intangible something alive in the heart of the storm; the trees seemed to be living creatures as they bent toward me, slapping their gnarled limbs at my face and tearing at my hair and eyes with claw-like branches. Finally, panting and gasping, I reached a small weather-beaten cottage.

The door hung open, revealing a scene of wild disorder. The furniture was scattered about, showing signs of a terrific struggle, and the lantern in the window swung wildly in each gust of wind. I called and searched the cottage to no avail. Once again, a strange feeling of the supernatural spread over me, and I was tempted to flee, but the prospect of sleeping in my cramped sports car was not pleasant. Also, I was deathly afraid of the storm and did not care to venture outdoors again.

Finding a few blankets, I attempted to sleep but found it impossible. The struggle that had taken place in this room haunted me. Somehow, I felt it was connected with the demon-like storm, and I feared the return of the creature that had broken in before—by now I was sure it was not of this world. Finally, toward dawn, I fell into a fitful slumber.

The noise of surf crashing on a rock-bound coast awakened me, and I arose, feeling cramped and stiff. I was surprised to find the ocean so near, as I had been unable to discern its noise in the storm. Looking about, the chaotic state of the room brought back the horror of the night before, in spite of the warm rays of sunlight pouring through the window.

I saw them when I went to the door; great tracks of some huge beast led through the uprooted trees and shrubbery toward the sea. They were at least half a foot deep and three feet long. With my heart pounding in my throat, I followed them. After crossing a strip of sandy, rocky beach, they disappeared into the booming surf. Seagulls, the only sign of life besides the tracks, wheeled and screamed overhead, as I stood on the lonely, forsaken shore and gazed, with horror, out to sea.

Turning, I ran away from the ocean, back to the road where my car stood. In a few moments, I had left the place behind, and rounding a curve, a tiny harbor village nestled among the cliffs came into view. After seeking directions, I was soon telling the desk sergeant at the local police station my story.

His face grew serious as he listened. "I should've known trouble was afoot last night from the sound of it," he mused. "We all warned that city fella, but he wouldn't listen. Knew it all, he did. Said our legends were nothing but old wives' tales —educated people don't believe that stuff and nonsense. Guess he found out different when he came."

"He?" I asked apprehensively.

"Yep. Guess you wouldn't believe it either though," the policeman said, noting my obviously city-bred appearance. "People like you and him that used to live there in the cottage don't believe in sea monsters."

• • •

If I were grading this paper now, I might give it a C+. Were adjectives on sale cheap that year? Could you buy clichés at half price? Was purple prose in style? I now believe Miss Hardy's grade was generous.

I saved "Storm B-" along with other high school memorabilia. I'd almost forgotten about it until Bruce Coville contacted me about submitting short stories to a series of anthologies he was putting together.

"The Grounding of Theresa" appeared in his *Book of Ghosts,* and "Give a Puppet a Hand" (now "The Puppet's Payback") appeared in *Book of Nightmares.* But what was I to submit for *Book of Monsters*? I'd never written about monsters. Or had I? I dug "Storm B-" out of my files and reread it. That B- still smarted, but I knew much more about writing now than I did then. Perhaps I'd write a story worthy of the A+ I'd craved when I was seventeen.

After a great deal of revising, I came up with "Trouble Afoot." I hope Miss Hardy would have liked the new version better than the original. At any rate, Bruce Coville included it in his *Book of Monsters.*

If you want to be a writer, you might learn something from the changes I made to improve "Storm B-." Any experienced writer will tell you that rewriting is the only way to produce a good story.

I'm often asked if I've ever seen a ghost. Maybe, but only once, and even now I'm not sure whether I was awake or dreaming. Late one night, when I was the only guest in a bed-and-breakfast place, something woke me. I was startled to see a man with his back to me standing at the window. When I made a sort of gasping sound, he turned and saw me. In the dim light, I noticed he was wearing old-fashioned clothing and seemed more frightened of me than I was of him. Before I could say a word, he ran from the room. When I told the owner what I'd seen, she said she was sure the house was haunted. She often felt benign presences and believed the original owners of the house were still there, keeping an eye on things.

I'm also asked if I believe in ghosts. My mind is open to the possibility. Several friends have told me about ghosts they've encountered, some in their own homes and others in well-known places like Harpers Ferry, West Virginia. I've also read many accounts of supposedly true ghost sightings, some of which are very convincing.

The problem lies in the nature of ghosts. They exist in a gray zone somewhere between life and death, in a twilight zone, so to speak. You cannot prove they exist, but you also cannot prove they do not exist.

After all these years, I'm still not known for bravery. Although I no longer fear the witch under the bed or the wolf in my closet, I startle easily. I'm uneasy in dark, lonely places. I don't read horror novels or watch scary movies. Often, my own stories scare me.

I have a theory that only people who know what it means to be scared can write a scary story. To scare others, a writer needs to know how being scared feels.

A story tells itself in its own way, in its own time. It can't be rushed. Or slowed down. Our minds play with it. Experiment. Change things. Take characters out, add new ones, reorder events. We're always looking for the best way to tell a story. A writer must be patient and try again and again until the story feels right.

But you know what? It might never sound right, and there's nothing worse than that. Sometimes the process of writing is worth the effort, even if we don't finish the story or don't like it. A writer can always go back to the story later and improve it.

You're already a reader. If you are a writer as well—good luck, and have fun!